"What do you want from me, Steele?"

Urgently he drew Judith flush against his chest. "You know what I want—" He groaned at the feel of her lower body pressuring his. "You. In bed."

She could barely breathe. "Me and the Great Protector, huh?"

"That's right."

"I don't need a man to protect me, Steele."

"Sully," he corrected, the tantalizing flick of his tongue coming after the hoarsely spoken name, sending delicious feelings swirling through her. "You said you'd call me Sully if I was good."

And he was good. Judith couldn't stop herself from wreathing her arms around his neck. Nobody had ever kissed her like this. Each thrust of his tongue was creating waves of internal pleasure. For so long she'd hoped a man would sweep into her life and arouse her in a way she couldn't deny. "Just kiss me."

His voice was almost a growl. "What the hell do you think I'm doing?"

"Talking."

"Not anymore." And with that he carried her off to bed.

Dear Reader,

Welcome to the third book in my BIG APPLE BACHELORS miniseries, set in New York City. While each book can stand alone, you'll remeet characters I hope you've come to love in previous stories. Now you're about to meet the oldest, sexiest Steele brother, a man who's known as *The Protector.*

Like his younger brothers, Captain Sullivan Steele is one of New York's finest and hails from a great city with a legendary heart. Sullivan is intense and passionate, and I hope his story will deliver everything I love about Harlequin Temptation novels—great sex, lots of emotion and a terrific happy ending that leaves you feeling good.

With all my best wishes,

Jule McBride

Meet all of New York's finest
in the BIG APPLE BACHELORS miniseries

Truman is *The Hotshot* in April 2002
Rex is *The Seducer* in June 2002
Sullivan is *The Protector* in August 2002

Jule McBride

The Protector

TORONTO • NEW YORK • LONDON
AMSTERDAM • PARIS • SYDNEY • HAMBURG
STOCKHOLM • ATHENS • TOKYO • MILAN • MADRID
PRAGUE • WARSAW • BUDAPEST • AUCKLAND

If you purchased this book without a cover you should be aware that this book is stolen property. It was reported as "unsold and destroyed" to the publisher, and neither the author nor the publisher has received any payment for this "stripped book."

To my favorite cop, David Shifren,
for serving, protecting and writing great novels—
not to mention being excellent company
during so many fine dinners

ISBN 0-373-25991-3

THE PROTECTOR

Copyright © 2002 by Julianne Moore.

All rights reserved. Except for use in any review, the reproduction or utilization of this work in whole or in part in any form by any electronic, mechanical or other means, now known or hereafter invented, including xerography, photocopying and recording, or in any information storage or retrieval system, is forbidden without the written permission of the publisher, Harlequin Enterprises Limited, 225 Duncan Mill Road, Don Mills, Ontario, Canada M3B 3K9.

All characters in this book have no existence outside the imagination of the author and have no relation whatsoever to anyone bearing the same name or names. They are not even distantly inspired by any individual known or unknown to the author, and all incidents are pure invention.

This edition published by arrangement with Harlequin Books S.A.

® and TM are trademarks of the publisher. Trademarks indicated with ® are registered in the United States Patent and Trademark Office, the Canadian Trade Marks Office and in other countries.

Visit us at www.eHarlequin.com

Printed in U.S.A.

1

A month ago...

"YOUR FATHER'S GUILTY." Framed in the doorway to the squad room with uniformed officers milling behind her, Judith Hunt stood before him, her posture perfect. She was wearing a gray silk suit with a jacket most people would have removed due to the summer heat. Farther behind her, through a window, sunlight glanced off the jagged steel Manhattan skyline in hot metallic flashes. "You know it," she continued, surveying him through suspicious blue eyes, "and I know it, Steele."

Steele, Sully thought. She usually used his last name, probably because she knew it grated on his nerves; on the rare occasion she used his first, it was always "Sullivan," never "Sully."

Standing behind his desk, he glanced down at the files littering the surface, his attention settling on a festive mug the officers had given him last Christmas. To Captain Steele: the Great Protector, it said, invoking Sully's nickname. The mug, when presented, had been brimming over with red-and-green condoms.

At least his men knew he was dedicated to ensuring safety. And unlike Judith, they had a sense of humor. Realizing with a start that she was scrutinizing his possessions, Sully shifted his eyes to hers again. He hated that he was reassessing everything now, wondering what conclusions Judith was drawing about him from the items, but he was glad the files made him look busy, which he was, and that she'd noticed the mug, since it showed his men cared.

The only thing Sully regretted was the ship in a bottle. Too personal, he decided. He'd built the ships when he was a kid, and he'd brought some into the office from a collection he'd otherwise divided between his parents' home and his downtown apartment. Built inside a Scotch bottle, the English galleon had five raised sails. It was from the late sixteenth century, with a sleek hull and low superstructure that rose toward a slate-and-teal-painted quarterdeck.

She arched an eyebrow. "A pirate ship?"

He shrugged with a casualness he never really felt in her presence, though why, he didn't know, since he was no stranger to beautiful women. Many times, his job had taken him into the homes of actresses and models. "Doesn't that figure?" he inquired mildly. "After all, my father's a crook, right?"

"I'm not sure a pirate ship's an appropriate ornament for the desk of a precinct captain," she agreed calmly.

"I find flying a Jolly Roger very appropriate, Ms. Hunt."

"The Jolly Roger?"

"Jolie Rouge," Sully clarified, the French words feeling sensual in his mouth as he nodded toward the ship. "A red flag. They were meant to communicate

that no quarter would be given. That any battle would be to the death."

"I'll take that under advisement." A heartbeat passed. "And thanks for the history lesson."

"No problem," he returned amiably. "Where better than a precinct headquarters to intimidate adversaries into surrender, to avoid costly fights?"

Judith knew very well he was referring to the near eruption of emotions that occurred whenever they met, which lately had been far more often than Sully would have preferred. "Is that what you're trying to do?" she countered, her lips twisting in a challenging smile. "Intimidate me?"

He fought not to roll his eyes. If Sully didn't know better, he'd think the edginess of these encounters was due to Judith's attraction to him. She wouldn't be the first woman to be drawn to him. "Would that be possible?"

"No. So if you're trying, it's not working, Steele."

There it was again. *Steele*. He'd worked with Judith ever since her transfer from the city's legal department to the investigative unit in Internal Affairs a few years ago, and now, for the umpteenth time, Sully wondered what made such a beautiful woman distrustful enough to spend her time prosecuting cops.

And she *was* beautiful—if a man could tolerate her attitude long enough to notice. She was nearly six feet tall. The hair hanging just past her shoulders was such a rich chocolate-brown that it appeared black. Her eyes were blue or violet, depending on the light, and framed by dark arching wisps of eyebrows. Her mouth, always highlighted by crimson lipstick, was so remarkable that it had earned her the nickname Lips. No officer said it to her face, of course, but the name was well-deserved. Sully wasn't the first to wonder how that mouth would taste.

She was clearly fighting exasperation. "Aren't you going to say anything more?"

"Why bother?" Sully asked dryly, pushing aside the tails of his brown suit jacket so his hands could delve into his trouser pockets. He'd rolled down his shirtsleeves, donned the jacket and reknotted his tie as soon as he'd heard Judith was on her way up to his office. This morning hadn't been bad, but the afternoon was heating up, and he'd just gotten a memo saying that the city, fearing brownouts as the heat worsened, was requiring that air-conditioning run low in public buildings. So far this summer they'd been lucky, but Sully's instincts told him this might be the last comfortable day. Right now, in the jacket, he felt as though he were being baked in a slow oven. It didn't help that Judith looked as cool as a cucumber.

"What do you mean, why bother?" Judith was saying, her voice a soft echo.

"I mean, when it comes to Pop, you've already played judge, jury and executioner. What's to discuss?"

Her crimson lips parted slightly, just enough that he caught a flash of her perfect teeth, a sliver of velvet tongue. The flattened palms of slender, manicured hands smoothed down the sides of her gray silk skirt. She was probably trying not to prop those hands on her hips, but the movement only served to accentuate the long-boned grace of her thighs. "The facts," she continued, oblivious of the effect she had on him. "Discussing those could keep us busy for quite some time."

Pulling his eyes from her legs, Sully said, "Given all the dirty cops you suspect live in this city, I figured you'd be busy enough without coming downtown to keep me company."

"Your lack of concern about my investigation into your father's affairs brings you under suspicion, Steele. And if you'll protect your father, Internal Affairs has to assume you'll also protect your men—"

"I am concerned," he countered flatly. He'd just come from a family powwow at his parents' home, not that he'd tell her that. Both his brothers, Rex and Truman, were cops, and they were just as intent as he on solving the riddle of their father's disappearance. "And nobody in my precinct's on the take, Judith," he added. He'd used her Christian name this time, and he was glad to see it grated every bit as much as when she called him Steele. Good. He'd keep using it.

She nodded curtly. "If anyone is, we'll find out."

Was she really going to use his father's disappearance as an excuse to crack down on his department? "Are you threatening me?"

Her eyes locked with his. "Should I be?"

"Are you?"

"I'm doing my job."

"And you're good at it," he admitted with grudging respect.

"If you think flattery will make me back off," she replied, as if he'd just confirmed every low-down, dirty suspicion she'd ever had about him, "you've seriously underestimated me."

He'd done no such thing. He knew Judith Hunt's résumé like the back of his hand—just as she undoubtedly knew his. "We should be working together on this."

She stared at him as if he were the most thoroughly dense man she'd ever encountered. "Which is exactly why I'm here," she said, not about to let him sidetrack her. "Joe wants—"

"Your boss is my father's ex-partner," Sully interjected, speaking of Joe Gregory. "They went through the academy together, then partnered up in Hell's Kitchen." After that, they'd begun busting gangs and mobsters in Chinatown. Years later, when Joe wound up working in administration at Police Plaza, he'd brought Augustus Steele on board. "Joe knows he's innocent."

If she had been privy to the previous connection between the men, she kept it to herself. "That may well be," she said, her tone dubious, "but Joe's the one who sent me to question you. He wants your father found—"

"I want Pop found, too," Sully interrupted, years of experience as a police officer enabling him to keep the indignation from his voice. "Because *when* he's found, he'll offer the explanation that'll clear his name."

"I want him found—" Judith's blue eyes turned steely in a way that indicated she knew more than she was telling "—so that I can prosecute him."

"In this case, you care more about making a collar," Sully accused softly, "than about discovering the truth." He paused, taking a calming breath. "What information do you have that you're not sharing?"

"None," she assured him.

He came right out with it. "You're lying."

"Steele, your father was caught on videotape, withdrawing seven million dollars in public funds. He transferred the money from Citicorp, then picked it up at People's National in two suitcases. The money belongs to the Citizens Action Committee—"

"I know that." Did she really believe he hadn't acquainted himself with the case? "It's a fund set up so citizens can donate to the police without raising questions of impropriety. Pop endorses and deposits the checks. It's a routine part of his job."

"Right. And the money's usually invested—"

"With the Dispersion Committee deciding where to spend it." Sully's own precinct had benefited from the fund the previous year, getting allocations for new squad cars. "Why wasn't the money invested?" Judith might offer him that much, at least. "Why was it available for a cash transfer?"

"Because someone was planning to steal it?" she said dryly.

Cute. "Not my father," he stated once more. "My brothers and I are convinced he stumbled onto an embezzlement scheme at Police Plaza."

Her eyes widened in astonishment. "You think somebody other than your father was going to steal the money?"

Sully nodded, choosing to ignore her sarcasm. "We think Pop withdrew the money, then hid it, so whoever was planning to steal it couldn't do so."

"Then why didn't your father contact Internal Affairs?"

"Because somebody at I.A. is involved?" he suggested.

Her soft grunt of protest did odd things to Sully's blood, both warming it and making it race. For a second, she sounded like a woman being pleasured in bed, an impression that was undercut by her words. "Steele, that's stretching. Your father's guilty. He took seven million in cash. It's a fortune in public money. No one would have let him take it from a bank, but years ago, he worked a mob-related bank heist at People's National, so the banker felt he knew him."

"The banker *did* know him."

"The banker thought he was *honest,*" Judith clarified.

"Pop *is* honest," Sully shot back.

Again she uttered that soft grunt that made Sully wonder if she'd sound like that while making love. If making love was the right terminology. After all, she was brilliant. She'd been at the top of her class in law school, and like many overachievers, she was tightly controlled, her manner challenging. Possibly, that control would extend to the bedroom.

Yeah, she was the kind of woman who'd let her mind get in the way of what her body wanted in bed, Sully figured. But then again, he could be wrong. Judith was also beautiful and inaccessible—a dangerous package. Maybe she was the type who was all-control until she suddenly let loose like an animal. Sometimes when he thought about it—which, of course, he tried not to—he imagined having hard, urgent sex with her. Hands roughly pushing up the hemline of her conservative skirts, buttons popping off blouses that covered small, firm breasts, panties trapped around thighs...

"About an hour ago, I met some eyewitnesses who placed your father at the Manhattan Yacht Club," she was saying. "They saw him there late last night, boarding a boat named the *Destiny*."

Realizing his mind had strayed, and that his mouth had gone dry, Sully pulled his attention back to the case. He nodded. "Right. That's the boat that exploded off Seduction Island early this morning. Did your informants say he was alone when he boarded?"

She hesitated. "Witnesses didn't mention seeing anyone else on deck."

"Could he have handled the craft by himself?"

"Is he good with boats?"

"Yeah. As far as I know. He likes to fish." It was the only outdoor activity his father enjoyed. Sully's middle brother, Rex, was a fisher, too, so it was a shame the two had never gotten along well enough to share the experience.

Judith was nodding thoughtfully. "If your father's used to fishing, he could handle the boat. It was sizable, but not a problem if he knew what he was doing. I'm leaving from here to take a team to the island. A Realtor, Pansy Hanley, says the explosion woke her. Maybe she'll remember something. The local PD's been diving into the wreck since it happened."

Rifling a hand through his short hair, Sully bit back a sigh as he thought of Seduction Island, a small key off the coast of New York, it lay to the south of better known harbors such as Martha's Vineyard and Nantucket. "My brother Rex is heading down there, also."

Judith stiffened. "Pardon my saying so, Steele," she said, "but it's awfully nice of me to come down and tell you what's going on—"

"Not really," he swiftly countered. "You said Joe sent you. You came here to get information, not give it, Judith."

"However, I *am* apprising you of the investigation."

Her tone was meant to remind him that she didn't have to. "Then please continue," he stated.

She didn't speak for a minute, and Sully suspected she was holding her breath and counting to ten. "I can't have you, Rex, Truman or anybody else interfering with my investigation," she warned succinctly.

Sully's temper was growing shorter by the minute. "Our father vanished," he reminded her. "He was aboard a boat that exploded. The Steeles need to know if there was foul play."

"You don't trust me to do my job?"

He set his lips in a grim line. If there was anyone he'd trust to get to the bottom of his father's disappearance, it was her. She was rumored to be the best, not that he'd tell her that. "That's not the issue, Judith."

She merely stared at him, her gaze cool. "If you Steeles withhold information, I'll arrest each and every one of you for aiding and abetting a suspect."

"He's our father, not a suspect."

Their gazes locked, and Sully couldn't believe the ease with which Judith maintained eye contact. Most people withered under the stare he'd perfected for years. Calculated to unnerve the hardest of criminals, his unflinching, penetrating gaze usually made people fidget immediately.

Keeping his voice low, still overcorrecting for a temper he was on the verge of losing, Sully said, "My father could be dead. You realize that, don't you? The *Destiny* exploded."

She nodded curtly. "We haven't found any bodies."

He knew that, too. According to one source, a sandbar off the coast was positioned so that Augustus's body might have washed up there, if he was dead. But Judith was right. There'd been no sign of any bodies. Nevertheless, Sully's gut tightened. No one in the Steele family would rest easy until Augustus was found. Rex and Truman were pulling out all the stops—Rex by heading to the island, Truman by calling his contacts around town.

Abruptly, Sully broke eye contact with Judith and circled the desk. For a barely perceptible second, she looked as if she wanted to back across the threshold, and when he stopped before her, her body became almost unnaturally still, as if she were determined not to react. The only thing Sully saw moving was the pulse in her throat, which he could swear was now ticking more rapidly. His attention lingered a second too long on a smooth hollow beneath her ear, then drifted down her slender neck to where pale gray silk draped creamy skin, looking like expensive ribbon on a velvet-wrapped present.

She might be one of the most beautiful women he'd

ever seen, but her personality, quite simply, sucked. "I'd like to know one thing," Sully couldn't help but murmur, coming an inch closer, just near enough that she'd feel his breath and the coiled power in his body.

She was tall, but not as tall as he, and because she was looking up, her wary stare came through a fringe of black eyelashes. He inhaled sharply, pulling in her scent. No woman had a right to be so beautiful, he thought vaguely, or to smell so good. Especially not a cop from Internal Affairs. And even less, a woman who intended to prosecute his father, something that made her the enemy.

"What do you want to know, Steele?" she finally asked.

"What happened that turned you to ice?" His voice had inexplicably hushed to a whisper. Suddenly, he was fighting the urge to lift a finger and touch her face—maybe because the gesture would send her packing. Or maybe just because he simply wanted to touch her.

Had Judith Hunt had many men? he wondered, his gaze arrested by her astonishing mouth. Had many hungrily captured those lips? Tasted their honey? Despite all the speculation, Sully had never heard of her dating. She always came alone to city events. She'd never married. But surely a woman this beautiful got a lot of offers. He imagined she dated higher-ups—the big brass from downtown, men with expense accounts and car services.

For a second, Sully almost believed he'd unsettled her. Her gaze faltered, but when she spoke, her voice was level. "Steele," she said, "I'm not made of ice."

"I said my father might be dead."

"I know that. And I have compassion for your situation," she added, her voice catching huskily. "I really do."

"Compassion?" he echoed. What did this by-the-book woman know about how Sully's mother was feeling right now? Did Judith know Sheila was just five blocks away, pacing around the courtyard garden behind the brownstone where Sully and his brothers had grown up? Or that Rex was giving up his vacation to join in the desperate search to find their father? Or that Truman was glued to a phone, questioning contacts, while Judith was planning her little jaunt over to Seduction Island? He'd never been there, but he'd visited vacation spots close to the New York shore such as Plum and Fire Islands. Even at that distance from the bustle of New York City, the waters of the Atlantic became crystal clear and cerulean.

"Compassion," Sully repeated dryly. "Oh, Ms. Hunt, I'm sure you've got it just the way they've got everything else downtown."

Her eyes turned watchful. "How's that?"

"In quadruplicates."

Her chin lifted a notch. What she said next seemed to cost her. "You're wrong about me, Steele."

He didn't think so, but he let it pass. They stared at each other a moment, and were still doing so long after other people would have looked away.

"If you think of anything..." Her voice trailed off, and before he could answer, she turned to go, a whiff of soft female scent cutting through the sweat of the squad room. She was across the threshold when she looked back. There was something odd about how she did it, too, Sully thought, because she glanced back the way a lover might, not an adversary. It was as if she had to make sure he was still standing there, watching her walk away. Her gorgeous crimson lips parted, as if she really wanted to say more.

He arched an eyebrow. "Something else I can do for you, Ms. Hunt?"

She looked at him another long moment, then shook her head. "Uh...no. But..." Her face was unreadable. "Look, Steele, I'll let you know whatever I can about the matter."

The matter. Hearing his father referenced that way was almost as unsettling as hearing him called a suspect. Especially since Augustus Steele was as straight as an arrow. He'd made the grade at Police Plaza, joining the crème de la crème of the NYPD, because that's where he belonged.

"Really," Judith added. "I'll let you know."

Sully doubted it, but he nodded, anyway. "I'll call you if he contacts me." That, too, was probably a lie.

She nodded back, curt and businesslike. It shouldn't have made fluorescent lights play in her dark hair, or intriguing shadows dance across her pale cheeks like whimsical phantoms. The things Sully was noticing about her at the moment had no place in a police precinct, but for a second—the space of a breath—he was sure he and this woman were going to wind up in bed. Like how the sun rose and set, there were just some things a man could take for granted.

And then the second passed.

"I'll look forward to hearing from you then," she murmured.

"It's always interesting," he agreed, then added, "Happy sailing."

She quirked a brow.

"On Seduction Island," he reminded her.

"It's work," she said, looking as if she was starting to have difficulty keeping her cool. "Not a vacation."

He wasn't sure, but as she turned to leave, he could swear Judith Hunt added a softly whispered, *"Dammit, Steele."*

That brought a smile to his lips. He watched her go then—his jaw setting, his groin tightening, his eyes sliding down the length of her. She was almost too thin, he decided. As willowy as a tall, thin reed, with small, high, firm breasts and slender, flat, boyish hips.

She was economical in her movements, yet possessed a curious lanky grace that would make her look good in things she'd never wear—feather boas draping across her bare back, floor-length black sheaths slit to her thigh, necklines cut down to her naval, tempting a man to glide a hand inside and push away fabric. Something timeless in her features made it impossible to guess her age. Twenty-five? Thirty? Suddenly, Sully had to know, not that he figured he ever would.

Realizing she was long gone, he mustered a long-suffering sigh, then shrugged out of the oppressive jacket he'd put on for her benefit. Loosening his tie, he muttered, "Can this day get any worse?"

"Probably, Cap." His right-hand man, Nat McFee,

stopped in front of him. "While Lips was here, we got a homicide on Bank Street, a three-car pile-up on Seventh Avenue, and Tim Nudel hauled in a suspect from that news kiosk holdup last week. You want to talk to him?"

Sully shook his head as he backed inside his office. "Nudel can question him. I need a minute." Maybe longer. He needed time to get Judith out of his system, and to mull over the string of bad luck hitting his family lately. "I haven't had a chance to breathe since I heard Pop disappeared."

"Why not take a walk?" McFee suggested. Before shutting the door behind him, he added, "Why don't you duck in someplace where the air-conditioning works?"

Maybe he would. Sully draped his jacket around the chair back, sat down at the desk and thoughtfully unbuttoned and rolled up his sleeves. *Pop's disappeared.* Sully could barely believe it. And he meant what he'd told Judith: he was sure his father had stumbled onto wrongdoing. Wherever he was, he'd return with the money as soon as he could.

Lately, Sully reminded himself, the Steeles had had some good luck, too. As if to reassure himself, he opened a desk drawer and pulled out a letter he'd written about a month ago.

"Only a month ago?" he murmured.

An eternity had passed since the day Sheila Steele had announced she'd won fifteen million dollars in the New York Lottery. That day, she'd made the even more astonishing announcement that she wasn't telling her husband, Augustus, about the winnings. Unless their sons married within the next three months, she'd sworn, she was going to donate the money to preserve natural habitats for wildlife in the Galapagos Islands. Furthermore, she'd stipulated that Sully, Rex and Truman couldn't tell their prospective mates about the money while wooing them.

"The Galapagos Islands?" Sully had muttered in disbelief when he and his brothers had retired to his childhood bedroom to discuss the matter.

"Don't get me wrong," his youngest brother, Truman, had said. "I've got nothing against sea turtles."

Sully had laughed. "Me, neither. It's the marine iguanas that get on my nerves."

"Oh, I don't know," their middle brother, Rex, had joked, "penguins are such a pain."

Marriage had seemed so unlikely for all of them, and it really did seem as though wild animals might benefit from the win. But now their little brother had proposed to Trudy Busey, a reporter from the *New York News*. Even more amazing, Truman, the brother most anxious to get the money, had vowed to give his share to the Galapagos Islands, anyway, so Trudy wouldn't think he was marrying her for anything other than love.

Sully sighed. Of course, *all* the brothers had to marry in three months or the deal was off, which meant the Galapagos animals would be the recipients. With Augustus's disappearance, everything had changed. Rex, who had no girlfriend, was heading to Seduction Island, and Sully...

He glanced at the letter in his hand. He'd written it the day he'd heard his mother had won, and while he was usually more cynical, the letter was like the ships he used to build in bottles—uncharacteristically romantic. It began: "Dear Lady of my Dreams..."

Sully's eyes dropped to the text.

Who are you? Where do you live? Why haven't I met you yet? If only I knew where to find you, sweet lady—which city blocks to wander, which cafés to visit. If only I knew what your face looks like...a face I'll hold between my palms and see resting on a pillow if you really turn out to be the lady of my dreams.

Are you out there? Maybe I'm too confused about what I want. Maybe I've passed you a thousand times without recognizing you. If I saw you, would I even know you? My last relationship lasted a long time, and she was in a helping profession, as I am. We had so much in common; we wanted stability and a reasonable lifestyle, to share our tight-knit families and have kids of our own.

But it wasn't enough. There was no passion. I don't mean sex, if that's what you're thinking. I mean...passion. There's no other word. I want my heart to race, my palms to sweat, my knees to weaken. Being able to remember love like that gets you through the hard times, and life being what it is, there are always hard times.

I'm a man who needs sparks and fire. Desire that compels. A person complicated enough to hold my attention. Are you out there, lady?

It was signed simply, "Yours."

The letter had been in the drawer for a while, but now, on closer inspection, Sully realized what he should do with it. At the bottom, he wrote, "I can be reached here," and left the address of an untraceable post office box, one he used in police work and for confidential personal correspondence. It was the address he'd given the lottery board, and just yesterday, they'd sent a questionnaire for him to fill out, apprising him of tax matters. Apparently, they were assuming Sheila Steele was going to turn her winnings over to her sons. The lottery board had no idea what Sheila Steele was up to—or had been before her husband disappeared.

Well, he was right to use the P.O. box, Sully decided. He was a realist and too suspicious to offer his home address. If he really sent this, it was hard to predict who might get hold of it and respond.

But he was going to send it. With a faint curl of a smile, he stood, circled the desk, went to a bookshelf and lifted an intriguing bottle he'd found in a junk shop during one of his lunchtime strolls through Greenwich Village.

"A genie bottle," Sully had pronounced, taking in the pale amber glass, round design and squat neck. He'd been thinking, as he often did, that he should start building ships again, and that this bottle would be perfect.

"Old," the shopkeeper had said, stopping to talk. "But not as uncommon as you might be guessing. I usually have one or two around the shop."

When he blew off a layer of dust, Sully imagined a trail of smoke rising from the bottle, as it might from a genie's lamp. Chuckling softly, he imagined the dust materializing into a woman. "Maybe it will," he murmured.

Rolling the letter, he inserted it and tightly stoppered the bottle with its cork. Returning to the desk, he lifted his jacket from the chair back, then headed for the door.

"McFee," he said to Nat as he passed the desk right outside his door, "I'm going for that walk you suggested."

"Anyplace special?"

Sully shrugged. He was the central player in this busy, West Village precinct, and it was rare he took time for himself when he was on the job. Still, no one needed to know he was strolling toward the banks of the Hudson. Already, he saw himself jogging toward the end of the Perry Street pier, drawing back his arm and swinging it in a wide arc. He saw the bottle fly from his hand, sail through the air and splash down into the choppy, brackish water. It would float a moment, then slowly sink, and once swallowed by the dark water, it would be caught in strong tidal currents and swept out to sea. Maybe a foreign woman would find it, someone as far away as Australia or China. Someone destiny would choose....

Before returning his mind to more pressing matters, namely his father, Sully tilted his head and considered. Wouldn't it be strange, he thought, if a woman really did find his message in a bottle and write him back?

2

The Present...

SITTING IN the underground parking garage, not wanting to leave her city-issue car for the sweltering August heat, Judith glanced at the blue suit jacket she'd folded beside her on the passenger seat, then stared murderously toward a glassed-in attendant's booth and a fire door leading from the garage into Sullivan Steele's workplace.

"The Great Protector," she muttered, turning off the ignition. "Yeah, right."

If Sullivan Steele had any urges to protect his fellow man, it was probably because he anticipated having those people cover for him if he ever got into trouble himself. Not that the Steeles didn't have stellar reputations. Around New York precincts, the men were legendary. The father had been in law enforcement for years, and all the sons were cops. Nevertheless, Judith had noted that good reputations often put a glossy finish on far less savory realities.

It was amazing what people got away with. Stable-looking homes with white picket fences often hid a world of trouble. That was the case, Judith supposed, with the Steeles. Sullivan had risen up through the ranks—with suspicious ease, in her opinion—to become the youngest precinct captain in Manhattan, so swiftly that it was rumored he was going to wind up in city government, maybe even mayor.

Oh, he was good at his job, but it was Judith's responsibility to make sure he hadn't greased any palms on his relentless climb. And while she had to admit he'd earned his position on merit, the family connections had to have helped. Somebody probably owed somebody a favor....

It was how these things worked. Still, she grudgingly had to admit that his men seemed to trust him. Why? she wondered, when it was so obvious he was protecting his father. She shook her head angrily. It took so little to make New York cops turn and look the other way. In fact, most people could be coerced to overlook wrongdoing.

No one wanted to snitch. The public moral code was to mind your own business. She sighed. At least the media wasn't making much of Augustus's theft—yet.

Vaguely, she wondered if Sullivan was right about her being too cold. But if she was suspicious, she had good reasons.

And she had called Sullivan practically every day during her stay on Seduction Island, as well as visited him during her overnights in Manhattan, hadn't she? Despite her show of goodwill, he hadn't been the least appreciative. As far as she could tell, it never had occurred to Sullivan that she'd phone him instead of using her scant free time to explore the peaceful idyllic island. But she shook her head. Given how close a clan the Steeles were, Judith wouldn't be surprised if he never talked. Whatever had happened, she was fairly sure he believed in his father's innocence. That, or Sullivan Steele was an accomplished liar, which, of course, some men were.

She cursed softly under her breath. Every time she thought of Sullivan, she felt tied up in knots. She wanted to believe he knew nothing about his father's disappearance, but she also knew she was on a case and couldn't trust him....

The middle brother, Rex, hadn't been any help, either. Her first day on Seduction Island, she'd threatened to prosecute if he continued interfering with the investigation. Then she hadn't seen him again until yesterday, when she was preparing to come back to Manhattan. Even though he'd pretended otherwise, she was sure Rex had remained on the island, searching for his father. Had Augustus been there? Had Rex found him? At some point, had the missing money been hidden on the island, as Judith now suspected?

She shot a rueful smile through the windshield, as if it were a crystal ball. Well, even if the money had been on the island, it no longer was. She hadn't told anyone, not even her boss, Joe Gregory, but she'd finally found it.

Her best guess was that Sullivan's father had withdrawn the money, then hidden it on Seduction Island. After a few weeks, Augustus had gotten paranoid, as criminals always did. Fearing the money would be discovered, he'd retrieved it and returned it to Manhattan. Judith had found it tucked away in a Manhattan savings and loan—in Augustus's wife's name, no less. Possibly, Augustus had blown up the *Destiny* himself, so people would think he was dead. That way, no one would look for him.

Complicated, yes. But like any knotted thing, the trail could be untangled. Over the past few weeks, Judith had slowly, painstakingly been working at the slippery strands. Now she was beginning to think Augustus Steele really was dead—not that she'd tell Sullivan that. But Augustus had been aboard a boat that exploded, after all, and then he'd simply vanished. What if he'd meant to fake his death, but had actually died in the process?

"Unbelievable," she whispered now. Her head was starting to ache from thinking too much. Apparently Augustus had stolen far more than seven million, since the account in Sheila Steele's name had recently swollen to more than double the sum missing from the Citizens Action Committee fund.

"Fifteen million dollars," Judith whispered.

Who knew how long Augustus had been skimming public money off the top? "A hundred grand here, a hundred grand there," she murmured. All nicely invested over the years—until Augustus's retirement neared and he decided to make a final heist and grab seven big ones—and more.

All this time, Judith's boss, Joe Gregory, had been suggesting she explore more intricate ways Augustus might have hidden the money. The idea that he'd simply rebanked it in his wife's name had never been considered. No law enforcement officer would do something so stupid.

Which was why it had worked.

It had taken Judith a month to figure it out. "The

Steeles sure live dangerously," she whispered. Especially Sullivan. At least he looked like the type. Her gut tightened as she thought of his imposing frame. Square-jawed, tall and broad-shouldered, he looked like a rich frat boy, except for his eyes. Too probing and intelligent, they set him apart from the macho cops who'd taken the job for their ego, because they liked carrying guns.

Sullivan was another breed. He reeked tenacity and competency, and yet Judith knew she'd be a fool to trust him. He aroused her curiosity, though, and even she could admit that the interest wasn't entirely case-related. Sometimes, in his office, she'd catch her eyes drifting over him, taking in the tapering V of his upper body, the flat belly beneath his shirt, and how the drape of his trousers accentuated long, well-muscled legs. A sudden shudder would ripple through her.

Well, today, no matter how his imposing physicality and challenging attitude tempted her, she wasn't going to tell him she'd found fifteen million dollars in his mother's account. No, Judith would patiently await the court order she'd filed, since it might allow her to delve more deeply, connecting the money in Sheila's account to that stolen from the Citizens Action Committee fund.

And presto, she thought. Her case would be solved.

Unfortunately, as her hand curled over the door handle, she felt a stab of unwanted guilt as she thought of the amber fire burning in Sullivan Steele's eyes. At times, she was utterly convinced he thought his father was innocent. If so, she was going to have to shatter his trust in a man he loved. She swallowed hard, since she knew better than anyone what shattered trust could do.

"Let's do it," she said grimly. The sooner she started, the sooner this would be over. Taking a deep breath, she grabbed her jacket, groaning as she shrugged into it. Leave it to Sullivan to force her to wear a jacket in this heat. But she simply couldn't go into his office without it. After all, he always wore one, even in public buildings, which were kept at temperatures approaching the boiling point.

As she lifted her shoulder bag, she realized it was unclasped, and a soft smile curled her lips as she impulsively plucked out an envelope. Suddenly, her heart missed a beat, skipping with excitement as she thought back to the day she'd found the bottle.

She'd been on the Perry Street pier, where she'd taken a walk after a predictably rocky encounter with Sullivan, when she'd first noticed the pale amber bottle caught in an eddy against the Hudson shore, kept in place by rocks and driftwood. Seeing paper rolled inside, Judith had gingerly made her way down the hilly embankment, despite the high heels she'd been wearing, and had lifted the bottle from the water.

She would never forget the magical rush of elation she'd felt when she read the letter inside. "Dear Lady of my Dreams," were the opening words, and the sender was like no man she'd ever known. He sounded sensitive, kind and passionate. Before writing him, Judith had put a trace on his P.O. box, of course, but she'd come up empty-handed, something she'd decided was good. Of course, if she really had to, she could flash her badge at the post office and get the information. She was just glad that, like her, the sender was cautious and self-protective, which meant he was a realist. She, too, had an untraceable box, though she didn't usually use it for love letters, but so that officers could report confidential information about their precincts.

This letter had been in her box today. Her eyes trailed over the words.

> Lady, can we meet? When I tossed the bottle into the Hudson, I imagined it being found years from now, by a woman in another country. I never guessed it might simply wash up on shore, and be answered by someone in New York, or that we'd start corresponding. Of course, we haven't gotten specific about the details of our lives—what we do professionally, or where we live....

Judith had intentionally withheld those details, and she suspected her pen pal had done so also, since details would make it easy to figure out their identities. Neither of them, it seemed, were very inclined to take risks.

Was she ready to do so now?

Her heart ached. After all these years, was a man about to come into her life? She'd never have sought that out; she'd been running too long from a background she wanted to keep buried in the past. But now...

No. Judith shook her head. She didn't dare agree to meet him. Pushing the envelope into her bag, she fastened the clasp, slung the strap over her shoulder, then stepped into the stifling heat. "I'm here to see Captain Steele," she announced when she reached the attendant's booth and pressed her badge against the glass window.

As he picked up a telephone, the attendant said, "I'll let him know you're here, Ms. Hunt." And then he buzzed her inside.

SULLY BARELY MANAGED to shrug into his jacket before Judith swept into his office, and having to put it on solely for her benefit was seriously worsening his already dark mood, if that was possible.

"You look cheerful," Judith remarked without preliminaries, her eyes traveling over the blue jacket he'd put on, as if noting it was the exact color as hers. Difference was, Sully thought, that the blue, while doing little for him, brought out the intense color of her eyes.

Telling himself not to notice, he said dryly, "Do I?"

"Just like one of those smiley faces," Judith assured him. "In fact, if they ever do a smiley face movie, Steele, you could be a body double."

"I'll have McFee issue a filming permit immediately."

"Really," she continued, "you don't look so hot."

"Quite the opposite."

The heat wave had turned his precinct into a madhouse, tempers all over the city were burning out of control, and he'd been putting out fires all day—quite literally, due to an arson case. It had been the wrong moment to hear that Judith was about to float through the squad room on those endless legs. Since he'd received a heads-up call from the parking lot, Sully had at least been somewhat prepared—as prepared as he ever could be for Judith Hunt—so had taken his time in studying her easy, unencumbered stroll across the squad room. By the time she breezed into his office, he felt like a member of the angry mob outside, not an officer trained to subdue them.

He shot her a sweet smile. "Well, Ms. Hunt, we can't all be blessed with your chipper demeanor, you know."

"Ah," she replied, her smile just as saccharine, the awareness sparking in her eyes making him wonder if she wasn't secretly enjoying the repartee, "wouldn't the world be a better place if everyone had my sunny disposition?"

That would be the day. At least she knew she was a control freak. What other kind of person would wear a jacket when the mercury shot over a hundred? "Have a nice time on your desert island?" He hadn't bothered to rise from his seat behind his desk—secretly, Sully was thinking he might faint from heatstroke if he did—and now he nodded toward a chair. "Care for a seat?"

"Thanks," she said, but didn't take it. "It wasn't exactly a vacation, Steele."

No, she'd been down there looking for his father. "Well," Sully conceded, "it didn't exactly turn out to be the most productive month for you, either." His brother Rex had fared better on Seduction Island, finding out their father was definitely alive. But Sully figured he'd keep that to himself.

Her chin reset defensively. "Excuse me?"

"You haven't found my father," he returned, wishing she'd sit. Every second she remained standing, insisting on towering over him, he was tempted to rise, and since he was sweltering, he'd much prefer to stay seated. "Are you sure you wouldn't like a seat?" he prompted again. "Believe me, I suggest it solely for my own benefit. If I have to keep staring up at you, Judith, I might get whiplash."

She almost smiled at that. Even worse, he almost instinctively smiled back. "So sue me."

"Maybe I will. Can I retire on a whiplash settlement?"

"How would I know?"

"You're a lawyer. I thought you all took that class in school—Whiplash 101." She still looked as though she was fighting a smile, and he was surprised to discover he liked the idea of that—Judith Hunt smiling. Had it ever happened?

"Bad hair day?" she finally guessed.

"Something like that," he said, rifling his fingers through the sweat-dampened strands.

She clucked her tongue, and for a second, his eyes were mesmerized by the crimson mouth. Even in this heat, her lip liner hadn't melted. "Poor baby," she commiserated, her mouth quirking. "Now that you mention it, Steele, I can actually see the gray."

"Better than a receding hairline," he retorted a bit defensively.

"You've got a point there."

He sighed, getting down to business. "I hear you gave Rex a hard time on the island."

Now that they were back on topic, she gaped at him, her bottom lip edging over the top, where sweat was starting to bead. It was Sully's only consolation. Apparently, in her ridiculously dressy jacket, she was as miserable as he. "Your brother was interfering in my investigation. I warned you before I left that if he—"

"He was looking for our father," Sully interjected. "Somebody had to do it."

"I was doing it," she shot back. "And if your brother found out anything, he didn't share the information."

"Information moves on a two-way street." It wasn't the first time Sully had said it.

"I called you. And I'm standing in your office right now. How much more goodwill do you want?" She blew out a short breath. "What have you found out since we last spoke?"

"Not a thing," he replied lightly, though he knew his father was alive. Sully wanted a chance to speak with him before he was found by Internal Affairs. "You?"

Looking as if the heat wasn't doing wonders for her disposition, either, she crossed her arms over her chest. "So, that's the way you're going to play today?"

"I'm not playing." Suddenly rising to his feet, he circled the desk, moving lithely for a man of his size, and then leaned against it. "You want the truth, Judith?"

Her eyes turned hungry. "Yes."

She thought he was going to divulge information

about his father. Instead, Sully said, "The truth is, it's been a helluva week. I'm hot and tired, and while it wouldn't be apparent to anyone on Seduction Island, the wheels of justice in Manhattan have ground to a halt because everybody's on summer vacation. I can't get warrants, and I'm battling a heat wave that's doubling the number of complaint calls."

"The whole city's having a heat wave, not just you, Steele. I'm trying to get courts orders, too. And if it bothers you so much—" she nodded toward his chest "—why don't you take off the jacket?"

Because she was wearing one. No doubt, this was Judith's way of finagling how to take off hers without losing face. "As a precinct captain," he said, shooting her a quick smile, "I have a certain image to project." *Image?* he thought. *Of what? A sweating pig?* Every man in the squad room knew Sully never wore a jacket unless the parking attendant called to say Judith was on her way up.

"Isn't it substance we need to concern ourselves with?"

"I guess, if you feel a lack of it."

"Which brings me to your father."

"Nice segue."

"Thanks." With a sudden sharp inhalation, Judith took him by surprise and did the unthinkable: she shrugged out of her jacket. When Sully saw the airy white, short-sleeved blouse beneath, he suddenly felt much more amiable. It was nearly transparent, and the white lace of a bra was visible beneath. The temperature in the room, already boiling, seemed to crank up another few notches, not that Sully minded now.

"That's why I came up to see you, Steele," she reminded him. "Your father."

He wished she had some news. Rex had found a man on the island who'd talked to their pop after the *Destiny* exploded, but nevertheless, Sheila was beside herself. Trying to keep emotion from his voice, Sully said, "Honestly, have you found something out, Judith?"

"Not really. After withdrawing the money from People's National, your father went to Seduction Island."

Sully's gaze drifted over her, as if seeking to pinpoint a chink in her armor, while she continued, "I traced the boat to the mob. The *Destiny* was owned by Tommy the Jaw. He was part of the Genovese crime family before he went legit." After a heartbeat, she added, "Supposedly."

"You don't believe he did?"

She shook her head. "Once dirty, always dirty," she pronounced.

His jaw clenched. "Just like Pop, huh?"

Her steady gaze seemed to confirm that that was her point of view. "Your father would have known Tommy from the old days," she continued. "Apparently, Tommy the Jaw loaned your father the boat."

"Or maybe my father's working with the mob," Sully suggested, his tone dripping irony.

Unfortunately, she actually considered that. "It's not far-fetched."

"Oh, please," Sully said, groaning.

She shrugged. "I found an abandoned estate on the island. The locals call it Castle O'Lannaise, after a pirate named Jacques O'Lannaise, who supposedly haunts it. I've got requests in for court orders also..." She shot him a brief look of sympathy. "I'm having trouble getting paperwork through, too. So it'll take me a couple more days to find out who holds the title. For some unknown reason, the information's protected."

Sully knew exactly how her mind worked: deviously. He never knew whether to be angry or impressed. Especially since his brain worked in the exact same way, putting them on the same wavelength. "You're thinking that, in addition to the boat, the property belongs to Tommy the Jaw and that Pop went to the island to hide out?"

"You're quick."

"If I'm ever worried about my IQ," Sully assured her dryly, "I'll know where to turn for an ego boost."

"Oh, not to worry," she replied. "If in doubt, just start with mine and count down a few notches."

"That's what I like, Judith. Your mature, seasoned wit."

She merely shrugged. "Castle O'Lannaise has been owned by a number of famous people in the past." The expression in her eyes turned serious. "The property's handled by a law firm, and even the Realtor, Pansy Hanley, doesn't know who owns it. It's been up for sale for a while, and now Ms. Hanley's got a buyer. The place is expensive, worth millions."

Somewhere in the neighborhood of four-point-five, according to Rex. Sully wasn't about to share the information with Judith, but it was Sully's brother who was doing the nibbling. While looking for Augustus on Seduction Island, Rex had fallen in love with Pansy Hanley and proposed. Once they were married, Rex intended to leave Manhattan, move to the island and use his part of the lottery money to restore Castle O'Lannaise.

Which meant, in addition to everything else plaguing Sully's life, the pressure was on for him to find a bride. How had his little brothers—two men with absolutely no prospects—gone from committed bachelors to being engaged in just a matter of months?

His mind straying even further afield, Sully thought of the letters he'd been exchanging with his mystery woman. Who would have imagined a local woman would find the bottle he'd tossed into the Hudson? Maybe this really was destiny. Maybe she'd be the one. The woman who was writing to him sounded so alive and passionate, and in his last letter, Sully had asked her to consider meeting him.

"Steele?"

He realized Judith was peering at him with uncharacteristic concern. "Hmm?"

"Are you paying attention?"

He refocused his attention on her. "Absolutely. I figure the money's hidden somewhere on Seduction Island," he speculated. "I figure that's why Pop went there, but your idea that he's in cahoots with the mob is ridiculous."

She hesitated. "I don't think the money's on the island."

She definitely knew something. "Why not?"

She hesitated so long that he felt sure she'd found some hard evidence against his father. Or at least something that appeared to be evidence. Judith wouldn't be this confident unless she'd found something she could use against the Steeles in a court of law. "What do you know, Judith?"

She shrugged, a lift of one delicate shoulder that shifted the sexy lace beneath her blouse. "Nothing."

Either the heat was getting to him or the lies were. "I think Pop hid the money on the island," he persisted, "to keep it safe."

"Oh really? I wouldn't have expected something so fanciful from an old cynic like you."

An old cynic? Was that what Judith thought of him? "You don't know anything about me," Sully found himself saying. His family was worried sick, and this woman was withholding information, playing games. "You see a suit and tie. What I look like behind a desk. Or when I give orders."

Her dark blue eyes were suddenly boring into his, vivid against the unbelievably creamy, pale skin of her oval face. "I see," she said dryly. "You're saying that Sullivan Steele—the man, not the cop—is different?"

It was exactly what he was saying. But how had they wound up in this conversation? Before he could ask, she said, "Your father's guilty, Steele. If you know that, but aren't telling me, then you'll wind up prosecuted. And if you don't know it, and can't accept it, I understand." He could swear her hard, crimson mouth actually softened, and for the briefest second, it looked kissable. "It's...difficult when people you love do something wrong."

The last thing he wanted was sympathy. "I want proof, Judith," he said, thinking she definitely wouldn't be this confident unless she'd found something. "Tell me," he demanded. "Why are you so sure he's guilty?"

"The videos that show your father taking the money aside?" she asked. "My sixth sense."

"Well, your sixth sense about the Steeles is wrong."

Challenge sparked in her eyes. "On that matter," she retorted, echoing his words, "*I* want proof."

There was only one way. "Fine."

She looked stunned. "You have proof your father's innocent?"

"Come over for dinner."

It was the last thing she expected. "To your house?" Laughter bubbled between her lips, and she gaped at him incredulously. "Dinner? Are you serious, Steele?"

It was the only way to convince her of his family's integrity. "Aren't you curious?" Unable to stop himself, he stalked closer, his voice lowering seductively as he edged in front of her. "Don't you want to observe the criminals at home?" he prodded, an almost playful smile tilting his lips. "See what we eat? How we interact?"

The interest in her eyes shouldn't have intrigued him, and when it did, Sully admitted that he sometimes wished Judith Hunt would express the sort of interest his mystery lady had. But with Judith, it was always the case. She'd phoned him from Seduction Island, and yet she'd never ventured anything personal—not even once. Didn't she have any human curiosity?

"You're inviting me into the den of iniquity, huh?" Her eyes locked with his. Maybe he shouldn't have felt quite so breathless when she said, "You're on, Steele. Name your time."

"Sunday dinner. We always have it at my folks' place." Everybody loved Sheila. This particular weekend Pansy Hanley was coming in from Seduction Island to see Rex, her fiancé, and meet and support Sheila. Truman and his fiancée, Trudy, would be there also. Sully gave the address. "Should I write it down?"

Judith shook her head. "I have excellent recall."

"Funny," he said. "Because you don't seem to be recalling whatever new information you've found out about my father."

The guilt crossing her features further convinced him she was withholding something. Given how he felt about that, Sully had no idea what compelled him to say, "Maybe I should just pick you up?"

"We'll see."

"You'll let me know?"

"Sure. One way or another, I'll see you Sunday, Steele."

As usual, he watched her go, this time mulling over how little they'd accomplished during this particular visit. Shrugging out of the oppressive jacket he'd felt compelled to don, he replayed everything that had just occurred. Judith definitely knew something, which meant he needed bargaining power. Sully hated to fight dirty, especially with such a beautiful woman, but this time it was necessary. He called to Nat, his desk sergeant.

"I want you to do some research on Ms. Hunt," Sully said when he appeared in the doorway.

Nat's lips parted in surprise, and he thrust a hand worriedly through the shock of wavy black hair that matched his sparkling eyes. "What are you looking for?"

"Anything I can use if I have to," Sully said simply. "She knows something about Pop, and I need to know what it is."

"But we're so busy around here—"

"No rush. Whenever you've got a minute."

"I'll see what I can turn up."

Good. Maybe by the time Judith came for dinner, Sully would know more about her. A vision of her blouse came back to him—open at the throat, fluttering against creamy skin. At one point, just beneath it, he'd glimpsed the cup of her bra, and like some horny teenager, he'd actually felt himself starting to get hard. He wasn't proud of it, but the moment had made him think of seduction. After all, Sully was extremely good at seduction...and seduction was another way of getting information from a woman.

"DINNER WITH Sullivan Steele," Judith murmured that night as she stepped from a cool bath. She inhaled deeply, enjoying the aromatic mist of her scented bath oil, as well as the fresh flowers she'd placed on the edge of the tub, using the amber genie bottle as a vase. "Have I lost my mind?"

Slipping into a white silk robe, she knotted it around her waist and headed for the living room, stepping on what had to be the greatest sin in Manhattan—a white carpet. Quite the luxury in a city where everything became dirty so easily. Vaguely, Judith wondered what Sullivan Steele would think if he ever saw it. It was tempting to bring him here, if only to shock him, since he obviously thought she was such a prude.

Trouble was, he was right, she thought, heat flooding her cheeks. Besides, because she didn't socialize much outside work, her nerves would be frazzled if he ever came here. Her correspondent, by contrast, wouldn't be nearly as unsettling a houseguest. The man who'd sent the message in a bottle seemed so kind and accepting, so willing to slowly build trust.

But now she'd been invited into the Steeles' world. Because Sullivan had invited her, it was a good guess that he didn't know his mother's bank balance had recently swollen to the unbelievable sum of fifteen million dollars. But then, this could be a ploy to make Judith *think* he didn't know his mother was probably involved in the Citizens Action Committee theft. Why else would she have so much money in the bank?

What if he really had no knowledge, though?

Guilt gnawing at her, Judith tried to imagine how Sullivan would feel if he discovered those closest to him were criminals. He'd be crushed. Fortunately, spending an evening with the Steeles would clarify things.

Passing a brocade sofa strewn with pillows, Judith

sat at a desk and withdrew the letter from her handbag once more. Her eyes trailed over the words.

> Lady, can we meet? When I tossed the bottle into the Hudson, I imagined it being found years from now, by a woman in another country.

The man sounded so heartfelt, so emotional. She sighed. So unlike Sullivan Steele. She got out a sheet of stationery, then merely sat there, pen poised over the paper, wondering how to reply. Searching for inspiration, she stared through a window at the busy street below and felt a sudden rush of gratitude for the milling crowds and honking horns.

Judith couldn't stand the quiet. Only Manhattan, with its noisy throngs, made her feel safe. There were always people here. A barely conscious voice played beneath her thoughts. *Always people to turn to for help.*

She'd come so far. She was thousands of miles from the farm in the Midwest where she'd grown up. Even now she felt a slight jolt of panic when she recalled the long road leading to the farmhouse, the isolation, how dark it looked at night with no other visible house lights.

She shuddered. For a second, the years between her and that house seemed to vanish, and she quickly reminded herself that she'd lost her accent, put herself through college and a law degree, and started over in this city of strangers. Outside, the countless lights—white headlights, red taillights and the cozy yellow glow from inside apartments—came together in a wash of warm color. Only then did Judith register that her vision was blurry because tears had filled her eyes. She blinked them back. She hadn't seen her mother or stepfather for years. Was she ready to risk betrayal and bring love into her life?

Pushing aside the question, she focused on two lovers below the window, happily holding hands as they walked along the crowded sidewalk. Her next thought was that Sheila Steele lived just around the corner. No doubt Sullivan lived nearby, too, since most officers, especially captains, lived in or near their precincts. In this city, he could have lived in the same building with Judith for years and she might never have realized it.

Sighing, she thought about Sullivan. He was thirty-seven. She knew because she'd checked his records, and judging by the hard glint in his knowing eyes, he was cynical and not getting any younger. Gray wisps painted the tips of the honey strands of his hair, and crow's-feet were visible at the corners of his eyes, giving his face a rugged, weathered look. He was sexy, too—sexy as sin.

But she wondered if she looked as cynical as he. Her eyes drifted to the letter again. There was a seemingly nice man out there who liked how her personality sounded in the letters she'd written to him. Was she ready to meet him?

At the thought, abrupt, unexpected pain seared through her. For an instant, all the trauma of her past came racing back, and she felt alone, betrayed and broken. *So alone,* she thought. As if the whole world had been hollowed out and she'd been left in the emptiness. Every time she started to hope someone might love her, she was filled with pain—because with the hope of that came the fear of loss. It was so hard to admit how much she needed love....

She hadn't mentioned her past to her correspondent, of course. She never would. But maybe she could open up to him just a little. If she didn't start making an effort, she was going to wind up like Sullivan Steele, unmarried and hardened by a cop's life. Guilt niggled at her again. Was her investigation going to shatter his trust in his parents? The way her own trust had been shattered?

She stared down at the letter again. If she agreed to meet her mystery man, at least she knew she'd be physically safe. She was well-trained in tai kwon doe, not to mention good old-fashioned street fighting. She also carried a gun.

Picking up a pen, she began to write.

Dear Mr. X,

I hope you don't mind the name, but I never know what to call you. Maybe you'll share your real name with me soon when we meet? Yes, I've given it some thought and think we should.

Pausing, Judith mulled over a date and place.

She wanted her next encounter with Sullivan Steele out of the way first, and because she was consumed with searching for his father, she'd be preoccupied the following week.

If I don't hear from you, I'll meet you on the Saturday after this coming one. At five-thirty in the evening, I'll be in Central Park, on the bridge in front of Bethesda Fountain, overlooking the boathouse. I'm tall, with dark hair, and I'll be wearing a red silk scarf, so you'll know who I am.

And then, her heart pounding, Judith quickly sealed and stamped the letter before she could change her mind. It was time to move on from her past. She'd learned how to survive. How to make a good living. She was at the top of her profession.

Now she had to acknowledge that love was out there in the world, just waiting for her. The magical experience of finding a message in a bottle had started to convince her of that. What an unlikely thing to have happen!

Judith could only hope she'd be able to meet her mystery man with an open heart.

3

"HAVE YOU CHANGED your mind about us Steeles yet?" Sullivan asked as he and Judith strolled along the stone pathway that wound through the lush, thriving courtyard garden his mother tended behind the family's three-story brownstone. By design, they'd dined late, after the sun went down, and they'd eaten dinner at a round glass table, where Sullivan's brothers and their fiancées were still talking with Sheila, sipping ice-cold margaritas until they felt ready for dessert.

"I came to observe," Judith said, "not draw conclusions—"

"How clinical. I feel like a lab specimen."

"You may not like it, but that's not far from the truth, Steele." The cold fried chicken and Waldorf salad Sheila Steele served for dinner had calmed Judith's nerves and mitigated her caustic tone, though not the words that came under her breath, so only Sullivan could hear. "And if anything, your lifestyle's made me even more suspicious," she admitted.

"Lifestyle?" He had the audacity to chuckle, and when the genuine merriment was undercut by the intensity of his gaze, Judith was reminded of their situation. Sullivan might be the perfect host, but he'd invited her here with an agenda—to get closer to her, so

he could monitor the case. "Does that mean you find more than our humble home suspicious, Judith?"

"Humble home," she muttered, slipping a finger beneath her hair to lift it off her neck for relief from the heat. "This is a mansion, Steele." She made a point of eyeing him. "And look at your suit." During dinner, he'd removed the jacket, but even wearing only a well-tailored shirt and tan, finely woven linen trousers that matched his hair and eyes, Sullivan looked every inch the king of the manor.

"My ex-girlfriend helped pick it out," he explained defensively.

"Good taste."

"Thanks."

She was more curious than she wanted to admit. "Ex-girlfriend?"

"Most men have them."

"Did she break your heart?"

"Since when did you decide I have a heart, Judith?"

"Be serious."

He considered. "We dated a long time, but..." Barely perceptibly, he raised his shoulders in a shrug, as if to say the relationship wasn't one he'd thought about in some time.

"Bottom line," she said.

"Not enough sparks." He lifted an eyebrow. "You? Boyfriend?"

"Never," she deadpanned, telling herself she hardly wanted to contemplate what *enough sparks* might mean for Sullivan Steele. Seeing his doubtful glance, she felt something unexpected and sharp pierce her insides. For the next second, it hurt just to breathe. She was beautiful; Judith knew that. She had thick dark hair, an arresting face and china-white, unblemished skin. Men had always chased her, many hadn't wanted to take no for an answer, and most had assumed she had a lot of experience, which she didn't.

For the duration of a heartbeat, she found herself wishing Sullivan was just a tad sharper, enough to see through her carefully erected facade. Deep down, that was her wish, wasn't it? she admitted, her heart aching. Didn't she want someone to break through her defenses and teach her to love again? *Pipe dreams,* she thought. In her experience men only got close enough to find out she was skittish around them, then they dropped her.

Sully was squinting at her. "Never?

When she brought her attention back to his face, she tried not to notice the soft, teasing light shining from eyes that were usually harder and more suspicious, and the playful lift of a mouth that was usually compressed into a serious line—at the precinct, anyway. "You're the one who's under suspicion, Steele, not me."

"And what have you found out tonight?"

She was still surveying those eyes, that mouth. "That you soften at home," she said honestly.

"Is that right?"

She nodded. "Like a teddy bear. But then," she added, "looks can lie. Besides, a cop's salary didn't buy all this."

He shot her a look of mock disappointment, shifting the subject. "So, your interest in my ex-girlfriend is strictly business?"

"What else could it be?" Judith rolled her eyes as they continued walking, surprised to find herself growing more comfortable in the summer heat and with the equally hot sensual undercurrents flowing between her and Sullivan. "Have you forgotten I'm trying to put your father where the sun doesn't shine?"

"You'll never get the chance. I won't bother again to say he's innocent. I'm starting to sound like a broken record."

"You're awfully sure of your point of view," she noted. "Haven't you heard—pride goeth before a fall?"

"I'm confident, not prideful. And I don't fall, Judith."

"Never?" she asked, echoing his words.

"Never."

He definitely looked confident. He *always* looked confident. "If you ask me, you're a little too smug tonight. Too self-satisfied. What are you keeping from me?"

He looked surprised, then shrugged. "I just found out I'm going to meet someone..." those amber eyes glanced away "...a woman with whom I've had some contact, but never a face-to-face."

"A work contact?"

He paused. "Personal."

Not about to give the impression that she was interested in Sullivan's love life, Judith decided not to probe, but she was caught off-guard by the sudden warmth flooding her. After all, she was in a similar situation. She'd just received a letter from the man with whom she'd been corresponding, and now his words played in her mind. *I can't believe you picked the bridge by Bethesda Fountain as our meeting place. When I was a kid, I learned to roller-skate there, and we—by we, I mean my parents and brothers—always stopped on that bridge for hot pretzels when we visited the Central Park Zoo. Believe it or not, when I'm stumped, I still go there, just to think. The bridge has been special to me for years....*

She felt the same way, but for different reasons. Years ago, when she'd first come to Manhattan, she'd stood there, staring down at the pond, fountain and boathouse, and she'd made hard decisions about her future. Then she'd walked down to the fountain and tossed in pennies—nearly all the money she'd had at the time—and she'd made the wish that had guided her ever since, to follow in the footsteps of people who fought for justice.

Realizing she'd let the musings about her personal life break her concentration, she continued, "You've worked with me for years, Steele. Did you really think a little cold chicken and Waldorf salad would make me lose interest in a case?"

"One hopes."

"Typical Sullivan Steele answer," she quipped.

So far, the evening definitely wasn't going as she'd planned. As it turned out, she actually liked Sheila Steele. And ignoring her protests, Sullivan had insisted on picking her up, as if this was a date. It *was* business, of course. But when Judith had seen how good he looked in the suit, she was glad she'd met him outside, instead of buzzing him in to her apartment, since that would have felt too intimate. She was glad she'd worn a simple pink silk dress, too. Sullivan had never seen her in anything other than a suit, and his reaction—a sharp intake of breath he obviously hadn't wanted her to hear—had been priceless. It had increased her anxiety about the evening, but had also made her feel she had an additional edge, one she desperately needed anytime she was near him.

Wondering how to get more information, she glanced around. Situated on Bank Street in Greenwich Village, the Steeles' home had turned out to be a massive brownstone that was gloomy from the outside, despite cheery green shutters. Inside, it was a cozy hideaway, largely due to Sheila's flair for color and design. A long, narrow hallway led from the front door to the back, then opened onto this incredible courtyard garden.

Despite the family's difficulties, Sheila had gone all out tonight—setting a table on the patio so that she, her sons and their dates could dine under a canopy of stars and leaves. She'd hung ferns and pale-colored Japanese lanterns from tree branches, and lit sand candles that flickered from inside pots along the walkway.

Since most trees in Manhattan were saplings planted in beds along the sidewalks, the trees here were particularly impressive—tall, with sturdy trunks, and wizened roots that ran along the ground before diving beneath the soil. Somehow, the exposed roots seemed apt, a visible reminder that the threads connecting the Steeles ran deep. But how far would each family member go to protect Augustus?

Shifting her gaze to some red marks etched into a trunk, Judith took in the boys' heights at various ages, then a sandbox that was kept filled, and decorated with shells. It was as if Sheila simply couldn't let go of things that represented a part of her sons' childhood. There was so much love here, such a strong sense of family history.

"A cop's salary paid for this?" Judith found herself repeating too abruptly, feeling a not entirely unpleasant jolt as her eyes met Sullivan's once more.

"This?"

She'd meant the house, but reached for the sleeve of his expensive shirt. The second she touched the fine fabric, she realized her mistake. She told herself to pull away, but while her fingers lingered too long on the buttery linen, she became overly aware of the stifling summer heat, the shadowy canopy of iridescent leaves and the muted voices of their dinner companions.

Unbelievable, she thought. Her fingers slipped to her side just as she and Sullivan stepped over an absurdly romantic footbridge; more for show than practicality, the decorative wooden arch curved over an electronically engineered brook that meandered through much of the garden. A plaster of Paris troll was perched beneath, and on the other side, Sheila had planted brightly colored flowers. The sheer romance of the place would unnerve anyone, Judith decided. "The house," she clarified. "And your suit. A cop's salary wouldn't buy it."

He didn't look offended, merely amused. "Maybe I pinch pennies. Shop sales. Cut coupons."

She held up a hand, palm outward. "Don't tell me," she retorted, forcing more sarcasm into her voice than she really felt. "You must have won the lotto."

"The lotto?" he echoed softly.

That he was ignoring her threats rankled. And yet his sudden laughter was so abrupt, unexpected and joyous that, like so many things about him, it caught her by surprise. Like the ships in bottles he kept in his office, that laughter seemed to provide a key to the real man beneath the exterior he showed at work. Listening to the rich sound emanating from deep within his chest, she tilted her head, wanting to like him. "You think I'm funny, Steele?" she demanded, hoping she didn't sound fazed by his sudden, inexplicable merriment over her comment about the lottery. "I'm not here to have a good time, you know."

He turned toward her, and while his eyes assessed her, she braced herself. His words still caught her off guard. "Do you ever?" he murmured, sounding genuinely curious.

In the dim light of the garden, his eyes, the exact amber color of the bottle she'd found floating in the Hudson, seemed mystically dreamy and yet unusually alert. The emotion in their depths was both intriguing and incongruous. With a start, Judith suddenly acknowledged that this was the last place she'd wanted to find herself: alone with Sullivan. "Ever what?" she managed to ask.

"Have a good time, Judith?"

"How presumptuous." She shot him a long glance. "Of course."

Conscious now of the hand he'd placed under her elbow to guide her, she felt it tighten, and despite her characteristic self-possession, she inhaled sharply. Somehow Sullivan had managed to use her elbow like a pivot, turning her.

Damn you, Steele, she thought as she faced him, her back coming to rest against the bridge's rail. Her gut clenched. No doubt he'd finagled this moment, intentionally stopping in the garden's most romantic spot. As he stepped closer, her heart hammered, and she silently cursed her voice for its soft catch of awareness. "What do you think you're doing?"

His not-so-innocent eyes skated down her face. "Hmm?"

"You know what I mean."

He'd gotten absurdly close, trapping her between his body and the railing, and the way the smooth line of his implacable jaw was tilting downward, he might well be considering kissing her. "Your father's missing," she said, glad her voice didn't waver. "Shouldn't you be thinking about that?"

He squinted down at her. "I *am.*"

"No," she corrected calmly, the accusation escaping before she could stop it, "you're flirting with me. You've been doing so all night." The spark of venom in her own voice took her by surprise. "Your mother set up a lovely dinner. Your brothers are on their best behavior, here with their fiancées."

"We're trying to show you a nice time," he said defensively.

"Maybe. But Internal Affairs keeps records on all Manhattan cops. So, before coming here tonight, I already knew your brothers by—"

"Reputation?" He scoffed disbelievingly. "Don't believe everything you hear."

"Truman's known as a hotshot," she cut in, "sometimes acting before he thinks. And I've met Rex. He's a master of disguises."

Sullivan looked incredulous. "You think that means you can't trust them? Judith," he said, sounding frustrated as he leaned nearer, "those are the very skills that make them such great cops. By the time I.A. gets through judging all the guys who are really out there in the trenches, getting their hands dirty and doing the job—"

"Spare me your views regarding my department," she interjected. "I don't think any of you would be so relaxed tonight—hanging around in a garden, sipping margaritas—if you didn't have solid proof that your father was alive and well."

She could swear he looked guilty. "Regardless of what's going on in our family, we have to eat."

"But here?" she managed to ask, wishing his near proximity wasn't making her chest so tight, her breath so shallow. "In...this garden?"

"Why not? The garden's Ma's pride and joy."

Judith glanced up at the sheltering leaves and fern fronds that shadowed the candlelit path. "Look, Steele," she said, "your mother seems nice, she does." Or she would, if Judith wasn't awaiting a court order so she could trace the sources for the fifteen million dollars sitting in her bank account. "I want to like her, I really do."

"You do?"

He sounded so hopeful that she exhaled an exasperated breath. "Of course I do. Your brothers, too, and the women they're going to marry. But you weren't exactly level with me."

"No?"

She shook her head. "I definitely didn't expect to find Rex and Pansy Hanley here *together*." It had been a month since she'd locked horns with Rex on Seduction Island. "He told me he was leaving the island," she added. Apparently, he'd stayed and fallen in love with the local Realtor who'd seen the *Destiny* explode.

"I should have mentioned that."

"Do you really think you're building trust by withholding information? Every time I catch you, it only builds up the case against you—"

"C'mon," he argued, "it was a minor infraction. And judging from the dreamy look in your eyes, I'm pretty sure my inviting you here has had some effect...."

"Steele," she protested, feeling a tug in her heart. "Yes. Of course it has an effect." The Steeles home was an ultimate fantasy land. Just looking around, she felt if a hand was reaching inside her chest, touching her heart. Sullivan didn't know—could *never* know—but this house possessed everything she'd dreamed of. She glanced toward the sandbox, then the tree where the boys' heights at various ages had been preserved. Did Sullivan have any idea how loved he'd been? Did he know how many kids weren't?

He'd edged closer. Without thinking, she planted a hand—instinctively, protectively—on his chest, then wished she hadn't. His heart was right beneath her palm. She could feel the strength of its beat, the curve of his muscles. Breath whooshed from her chest. "Look," she muttered. "This place is amazing." She could admit that much. "Seductive." With every breath, she drew in floral scents that made her head reel.

He was watching her carefully, and when he spoke, his voice was low. "Did you just say seductive, Judith?"

"Yeah." Her breath was coming out hard and shallow; no doubt he noticed. "You know, Steele. Flowers and candlelight."

His eyes were boring into hers now. His face angled downward another inch, and just when she was sure he meant to brush his lips across hers, he halted. His voice came out sounding hoarse. "Don't forget the moon, Judith. That's shining, too."

She loosened her hand, so that only her fingertips remained on his shirt, and stared right back at him. "Where'd all your money come from?"

"I take it moonlight makes you uncomfortable," he murmured.

"Let's switch the subject. In the interest of being a great host and accommodating a houseguest, why don't you tell me where your money comes from?"

During the long moment he considered, Judith had the distinct impression his mouth was about to swoop down and capture hers. But surely even Sullivan Steele wouldn't go that far, would he?

"Ma's family had money." His tone turned deceptively mild, and he leaned away, just far enough to push aside a swaying fern frond that threatened to brush her cheek. Grasping her hand as though it was the most natural thing in the world, he started walking again. "She inherited it."

The light touch of Sullivan's fingers threading through hers had taken Judith's breath. "Inherited?" she managed to say.

He dropped her hand when they reached the other side of the footbridge, and when he leaned down, plucked a daisy from the grass and handed it to her, she bit back another curse. "You're not going to charm me," she warned as she slipped the flower into the top buttonhole of her dress.

He merely smiled. "We'll see about that."

At least she was getting information, she told herself. That was the important thing. It was just too bad Sullivan's breath was still feathering across her cheek, and that his hip kept grazing hers as they matched their long strides.

"Her family didn't much like it when she married a cop," he explained, heading toward the dining table, seemingly oblivious of the fact that he'd almost kissed her. "Pop was just out of the police academy at the time. Ma's folks are upper-crusty, live out in the Hamptons. East Hampton," he clarified.

She'd have to check that out. "She's wealthy?" When her heart skipped a beat, Judith realized how much she wanted the Steeles to be cleared. Possibly the incredible amount in Sheila's account was legitimate.

But he shook his head. "Not anymore. If my folks didn't lease some of the rooms in the house, they couldn't afford to live here. Ma only inherited the house. There was nothing left over for upkeep."

Did that explain why Augustus had stolen so much money? To help save his wife's family home? Just as the dining table came into view, Sullivan grasped her hand again. "C'mon. I invited you here to show off our good side. Can't you quit working?"

She didn't know whether to be amused or annoyed by his persistence. "No."

"Well, it is one of the things I like about you."

She lifted a brow. "I wasn't aware there were any."

"There are a few."

"Such as?"

He smiled. "I never thought I'd see Judith Hunt fishing for compliments." When she said nothing, he added, "Tenacity. I like that. You're not a quitter, Judith."

It was truer than he knew. She thought of her background, how little she'd had to work with, and how hard she'd fought to keep going without money and support.

"And you're beautiful."

Stiffening, she realized she had to get away from this man. It wasn't her imagination. He was trying to seduce her, and she was going to get hurt. "One more word, and I'll consider it proof that you're sweet-talking your way into my investigation," she warned.

"Step lightly, Steele, or I'll fine you for obstruction of justice."

When he made a point of tiptoeing on the path, she couldn't help but laugh. His ploys were working, she decided. She kept circling around him, hoping he'd crack and tell her what he knew. But she'd also...come to want contact with him, hadn't she? Wasn't that one of her motives? Swallowing hard, she wondered if Sullivan suspected she was attracted to him. "Thanks for the walk. The garden's lovely."

Fortunately, they'd reached the dining table, and Truman's fiancée picked up the conversation. Trudy Busey was petite and lively, with blue eyes and a bouncing blond bob, and Judith couldn't help but think she was exactly the kind of high-energy woman who'd be able to keep Truman Steele in check. "We're thinking of creating a coffee table book," she enthused, threading her fingers through her soon-to-be husband's.

"Trudy thinks the garden's romantic," Truman clarified, thrusting his other hand under his light brown hair, to get it off his neck, and surveying Judith through whiskey-colored eyes very like his big brother's.

"Pictures of the garden would be terrific in a book," Judith agreed, deciding she liked Trudy immensely.

"Another margarita?" asked Rex.

"Sure," said Judith.

As he poured her a glass, she realized Sheila was watching her through kind eyes. They were dark like Rex's—the other two men took after their father—and Sheila's hair was prematurely gray. She'd drawn it atop her head tonight and wore a casual batik shift printed with bright flowers.

"Dinner was amazing," Judith said as Sullivan reseated her at the table. "I never have time to cook."

Sheila laughed. "Are you kidding? In this heat? I ordered from Giovinchi's. It's around the corner."

"Yes, she's been too busy to cook for us," complained Rex, as his mother rose from the table. "She's been doing so much volunteer work for C.L.A.S.P." He glanced at Judith. "That stands for City and Local Activists for Street People."

"Mothers who care about their children cook," teased Truman, shooting his mother a self-pitying glance as she headed for the door.

"I made the dessert," she retorted over her shoulder as Pansy hopped up from the table to lend a hand. "I'm going to get it right now. Pansy and I whipped up the margaritas you're drinking, too."

"Delicious," pronounced Judith, taking a deep draft from the salty rim of the glass. She didn't usually drink, but given the heat, the margarita was more than welcome. Besides, it didn't taste as if it had any alcohol in it, and while Trudy Busey chattered about stories she was writing for *New York News*, Judith finished it and started another.

"So that's how Truman and I solved the Glass Slipper Case," Trudy finally finished, after detailing the story of how she and Truman had fallen in love. "I'm also close to identifying the missing winner of the New York Lottery," she said with a mysterious smile that vied with the Mona Lisa's, "and following up on an oil spill, from a ship called the *Eliza.* It went aground near the Galapagos Islands."

"I just want to get married," said Truman with a laugh.

"We want to," Trudy put in. "Just as soon as—as..."

Augustus Steele was found.

The words hung in the air, as they had through the evening, and the tension was suddenly palpable. All night the Steeles had been overly chatty, and Judith felt sure it was for her benefit. That, or they really did have information that Augustus was alive. If so—and if he really was innocent—wouldn't Sullivan have told her? She shifted uncomfortably, suddenly wondering if the margaritas contained more alcohol than she'd suspected. Then she noticed that Sullivan's arm was draped casually across the back of her chair.

"I keep trying to tell Trudy I'm not going anywhere." Truman plunged on, abruptly recovering the moment. "But she's hell-bent on marriage. She won't feel safe until the ring's on her finger."

"I want to get married right here," she said breathlessly, "in this garden. And Rex and Pansy have dibs on Castle O'Lannaise."

"The big estate on Seduction Island?" asked Judith, the mention of it jarring, since she suspected Augustus Steele might have hidden there with the money he'd stolen. But then, maybe not. Anyway, while the place needed some work, Pansy was right. It would be perfect for a wedding.

Judith glanced toward Rex's fiancée. Pansy was less take-charge than Trudy. Long honey-colored hair fell past her shoulders, cut in airy wisps, and her shorts and sandals were in direct contrast to Trudy's more urban look. "In order to get married there," Judith said, "you'll probably have to find out who owns the estate."

Pansy flushed with what might have been guilt. "I've got the listing for it, but as I explained when you were investigating on the island, I'm not sure who the owner is...."

Trudy was still on her own wavelength. "I...think I'm going to invite my mother to the wedding," she said, then explained that she and her mother, Marcia Busey, had been estranged for years, and that Trudy had been raised by her father. "My mother's a talking head for a TV station in Birmingham," she finished.

So, her mother had chosen a career over child-rearing. Judith's heart ached as she thought of her own mother, whom she hadn't seen for thirteen years. And never would again. Judith wasn't proud of it, but turbulent emotions still lingered. Despite the impossibility of reconciliation, she sometimes felt an urge to be in touch, not that she'd act on it. Judith had more strength and perseverance than that. God help people who turned their backs on their children. Her voice softened. "You think your mother will come?"

"I don't know," Trudy said with a shrug. "I haven't contacted her yet, but I thought it would be nice. My father will be mad, but it's time he came to terms with the past."

She threaded her fingers more tightly through Truman's as she launched into a lighter, more humorous story about her sisters-in-law, whom she'd asked to be bridesmaids. "It'll be the first time they've ever worn shoes without bows on the toes," she quipped. "I'm also banning headbands with polka dots."

Pansy groaned as she and Sheila circled the table, putting down dessert plates of cool flan. "I dread seeing what Vi will wear," she said, speaking of her youngest sister, while encouraging everyone to start eating with a wave of her hand. "She's a total klutz when she gets nervous," she explained, as she reseated herself and dug into the flan, "so I expect she'll ruin whatever she puts on. My other sister, Lily, lives in string bikinis, so if I can get her to wear any dress at all, I'll consider myself lucky."

Grinning at Rex, Pansy continued. "The ceremony's going to be on Seduction Island at Castle O'Lannaise, and we're going to read our own vows. Rex writes the most romantic poetry...."

"Careful," Judith said between bites, trying to ignore how Sullivan's arm was dipping downward on the chair back, coming closer to her shoulders, "or you'll ruin the macho cop image." Earlier, Sullivan had given her the grand tour of their childhood bedrooms, and once more she'd been astonished by the intricate ships he'd so painstakingly built. Now, for the first time, she noticed the delicacy of his hands. They were large, yes. And very masculine. But his fingers were long and slender, the hands of an artist. She couldn't help but imagine how they'd feel, gliding along her skin.

"Well," Rex was saying, "I'm quitting the force, anyway."

That took her by surprise. "To...?"

He shrugged, glancing at Pansy. "I don't know," he said cryptically, lights dancing in his eyes. "Maybe run a hotel. Paint on the beach."

"So, you're relocating to Seduction Island?"

Rex smiled. "Yeah. To be with Pansy."

Such a lifestyle took more money that an officer could save, but Judith kept the thought to herself.

"I just hope your father comes home," Sheila murmured.

"Now, Ma," chided Sullivan, who'd eaten with lightning speed and was now polishing off the last bite of dessert. "We said we were going to keep it low-key tonight."

With a start, Judith realized once more that the light mood had been engineered solely for her benefit. "Not on my account, I hope. I wouldn't want you to—"

Sheila shook her head, her hand instinctively closing over Judith's, making Judith's chest tighten. The gesture was so sweet, natural and maternal. It was impossible not to warm to this woman, and yet the fact remained that there was fifteen million dollars in her bank account—money she apparently hadn't inherited from her East Hampton relatives.

Earlier, shortly after Judith and Sullivan arrived, Sheila Steele had pulled her aside, patted her arm and said, "I know you're looking for my husband. I know you suspect him of being a criminal, too, but it's not true."

"Your sons clearly feel the same," Judith had murmured.

Not then or since had she felt she'd come into enemy territory. Despite whatever was happening with Augustus, these people continued to believe he was alive and innocent. The *Destiny* had exploded weeks ago, and yet they hadn't given up hope.

Judith eyed Sheila now, unsure what to think. Her best guess was that Augustus had stolen the money, left Manhattan with it, then returned and deposited it in the bank, in his wife's name, and that Sheila was unaware of it.

To break the tension, Judith turned her attention back to the garden. "This is a wonderful place," she murmured. "You've made the kind of home your children want to come back to."

Sheila's gaze was sharp, perceptive, but without malice, and now her eyes filled with concern. "Are you out of touch with your family?"

Usually more circumspect, Judith found herself shaking her head. "We...don't have a lot of contact." Actually, they didn't have any.

"And where are you from?"

She hesitated, aware that Sullivan was listening with rapt attention. "The Midwest. Oklahoma."

He frowned. "I didn't know that."

She glanced at him as Trudy rose and started removing the dessert plates. "Why would you?"

"I..." He suddenly chuckled, his mouth quirking. "Honestly, I thought you were from one of the boroughs. Queens or Brooklyn. You don't have an accent, but you seem like a city girl."

"Woman," she corrected, and wished she hadn't, since the slow drop of his appreciative male gaze seemed to say she was every inch that. "I'm glad I fit in," she added.

"You do," he said simply, but this time, he seemed to be referring to how she'd gotten along with his family, not in Manhattan. His gaze lingered, and she was sure he was noting her clothes, hair and nails. She was tastefully turned out, and her jewelry, what little there was of it, was discreet, as was most of her makeup. Except for the crimson lips that were her signature. Sullivan Steele didn't have to know that her law school roommate had been a trust-fund baby who'd seen Judith's potential and taken her under her wing, showing her how to better fit in.

He was still frowning. "Where'd you go to law school?"

Again she hesitated. "Harvard."

Sullivan eyed her, looking almost as if she'd intentionally withheld information from him, which was rich, given that he hadn't even bothered to mention the connection between Rex and Pansy Hanley. "I didn't realize you had..."

"That kind of pedigree?" She didn't want him to think it, either. She'd worked too hard. "Scholarship student."

"And you went into Internal Affairs," he mused.

The implication was that she could have used the degree in private practice. "Yes," she conceded.

He raised an eyebrow that looked golden in the candlelight. "You just had a yen to prosecute the good guys?"

She swallowed hard. Sullivan definitely knew how to cut to the chase. It was almost as if he knew there was one particular good guy out there from whom she hadn't gotten satisfaction. "I only prosecute the good guys who turn out to be bad."

His voice turned strangely lazy. "What about the bad guys who turn out to be good?"

He was speaking of himself. "I never said you were bad."

"*Au contraire.* Haven't you ever heard it's not good to lie to a cop?"

She shrugged, a slight smile lifting her lips. "I didn't see a polygraph around." Because the curiosity in his gaze worried her so much, she added, "Speaking of work, it's been a long day." She smiled around the table, her eyes lingering on Sheila Steele. "I should probably get going...."

Sullivan rose.

"No, please," she stressed. "You picked me up. Why don't I take a cab? Stay and enjoy the rest of the evening."

"I've got to be at the station by five tomorrow morning."

She smiled appreciatively. She had to give the man that much; he had impeccable work habits. "Well..." Not seeing a way to get out of letting him take her home, she stood in turn and said her goodbyes, then she and Sullivan walked toward the back door of the house, the soft sudden brush of his thigh against hers bringing a swift, unexpected rush of heat.

Feeling sure she'd never come here again, she paused when they reached the door, and looked back, casting a glance over the lush, wonderful leafy plants and arbors, the baskets of thick ferns that draped the walkway, the Japanese lanterns and glimmering sand candles. It was impossible at the moment to think that in just a minute, they'd walk through a long hallway and find themselves out on Bank Street again, and then on Hudson, which was even busier, with throngs of tourists.

"It's really lovely," she murmured, her eyes sweeping over the romantic scene. "And it's surprising to see such a place in Manhattan. I usually don't care much for peace and quiet."

It might have been the most revealing thing she'd ever said to him. "You don't?"

She shook her head quickly. God no. It reminded her of the farm. Of all those acres, and the darkness of the evenings. Of how the nearest house was miles away. She pushed away the rest of the thoughts that came. "I like having people around."

"Me, too." He flashed an easy smile, but it didn't reach his eyes; he'd registered her discomfort. "I grew up in the city. Oklahoma must have been—"

She didn't want to think about Oklahoma. "It's late. We'd better get going." Still, she couldn't pull her eyes from the soothing garden.

"This need not be the only time you come here, Judith," he said, as if reading her mind, and his voice, like his suit, seemed suddenly, strangely formal. For a second, everything seemed crazily, dangerously romantic. She felt as she had years ago, before she'd been so desperately hurt, back when she'd believed a prince had come into her world and swept her off her feet like a fairy princess.

The sound of jingling car keys brought her back to

the present. Tonight Sullivan had played the gentleman, opening doors, pulling out chairs, nearly kissing her. She doubted it meant anything special, since Sheila Steele was the type who'd raise men to treat a woman with respect. Still, tonight had felt special. Because she was around macho cops most of the day, many of whom she was prosecuting, Judith didn't exactly get the royal treatment. Usually, doors shut in her face.

Mulling over everything she'd seen, she felt even more confused than before. Despite their very comfortable lifestyle and the money in Sheila's account, the Steeles really did seem as aboveboard as the reputations that preceded them. Sheila had bucked up, determined to show her guests a good time, but she was deeply in love and worried about her husband. None of them, Judith would wager, knew that fifteen million dollars was in that bank account. She sighed, pondering her next move, then realized Sullivan was carefully watching her.

"Ready?"

She nodded.

When he slid a hand over her waist and opened the door, she felt as if she was on a good old-fashioned date, where a man had taken her home to meet his mother. Drawing a sharp breath, Judith tried to deny how her mouth went dry, her pulse quickened and a cold drop of sweat glided down between her shoulder blades.

She wasn't sure if it was from fear or desire. Not that she could indulge either, especially not desire. She was out to prosecute Sullivan's father. Besides, she was about to meet the man with whom she'd been corresponding, a man who was so much tamer and safer than Sullivan. And more than anything, Judith needed a man to be safe.

Nevertheless, she *wanted* Sullivan.

"Ready?" he asked again, breaking into her reverie.

"Yeah," she managed on a slow whoosh of breath. And then she thought, *Romantic gardens be damned. No way is this night going to end with Sullivan Steele kissing me.* And then another telltale shiver claimed her, making her realize she was probably wrong.

4

As soon as he stepped inside Judith's apartment, Sully knew he shouldn't have. Being here felt too personal, too intimate. When he'd asked Judith to share more notes about his father's case, he hadn't expected her to comply, but surprisingly, she'd invited him upstairs. Now, as she turned away and bent to rifle through some file folders, Sully settled his eyes where the pink silk hem of her dress was rising upward on bare thighs. When he took in the hollowed backs of her knees, something harsh and dry hit the back of his throat.

Torture, he thought. *Pure, relentless torture.*

Earlier, he'd almost kissed her in the garden. Their lips had been a breath apart. Right now, he still wanted nothing more than to claim her mouth. What would she do? Protest, maybe? A slight smile tugged his lips. *Call the cops?*

Or would she let him? A deep sigh of anticipation rumbled in his chest. Yeah, he could almost see himself savaging her lush mouth, plunging his tongue between the crimson lips she was so well known for.

The dress she'd worn tonight was nothing like her prim suits. The straps were thin—so thin she couldn't wear a bra—and all night he'd caught himself looking, his gaze tracing small, firm, high breasts. In a flash fantasy, he saw his large hands curling over them, and he imagined how the tips would look—duskily dark and achingly tight—as he rolled them between his fingers. In his mind's eye, he circled a thumb around an aroused nipple, lifting it so he could suckle.

He blew out a shaky breath. No doubt about it; tonight had been too much. He and Judith never should have stepped outside the safe confines of a precinct. Out here, in the real world, things could get a lot more complicated. Sure, he'd thought of seducing her to get more information as she worked his father's case, and yes, he'd asked Nat to snoop into her background, but now that Sully was standing in her personal space, he was starting to doubt his own wisdom.

He took a sharp breath, then wished her perfume hadn't come with it, knifing into his lungs. For another long moment, he continued looking his fill, leisurely perusing the soft fabric that nipped in at her waist. It molded over her backside, just the way his hands wanted to.

She looked good enough to eat. Literally. And the apartment wasn't bad, either. All-white carpet. Chic onyx colored furniture. Built-in TV. "Guess they pay I.A. officers more than no-account precinct cops like me," Sully said dryly as she turned around.

"Guess so, Steele," she returned airily, striding toward him on long legs that he now imagined wrapping around his waist. "Jealous?"

"Green with it."

"Good."

"You always enjoy a man's discomfort?"

"It's one of my favorite pleasures in life."

How could such an annoying female excite him? The woman with whom he'd been corresponding was going to meet him next Saturday. In her letters, she sounded so much less complex than Judith, but while Sully tried to convince himself that was a good thing, he also knew it was a lie. The way Judith Hunt went head-to-head with him fired his blood and left him edgy. He was quicker when he was around her, his mind ticking, his senses heightened. Wasn't that what men really wanted in a woman?

He shook his head to clear it. With his father missing, he shouldn't be thinking this much about the fairer sex. He and his brothers needed to concentrate on finding Augustus.

Still, Truman and Rex were getting married, which meant Sully's lack of a bride was the only thing standing between the brothers and sharing their mother's fifteen-million-dollar lottery win. He pushed aside the thought. What the hell was he contemplating, anyway? Marrying Judith Hunt? *Get real.*

His hand grazed the back of Judith's as he took the file folder, and while something so simple shouldn't have sent sparks through him, it did. He registered the softness of her skin, its warmth in air-conditioning that was affecting her breasts, making them go noticeably taut.

She cleared her throat. "Here are the notes you wanted...."

She'd caught him looking, and just the increased sharpness in her arresting blue eyes made him want to kiss her again. No doubt she'd registered the heat in his eyes, too, because she glanced away suddenly, as if the tension was too much to bear.

"Don't look so hungry, Steele," she added, her voice remarkably steady as her gaze returned to his. "The notes are nothing confidential."

The notes had nothing to do with why he looked so hungry. "Maybe you saw something that will spark my own ideas about wherever Pop went."

"Well, they're just some of my thoughts while I was on Seduction Island, going through what was left of the boat after it exploded." She paused. "And for what it's worth..."

He waited, feeling powerless as his eyes inadvertently drifted downward again, his gaze grazing the front of her dress. "Yeah?"

"I liked your family, Steele."

The comment felt more significant than it should have. He felt a twinge of something else, too—curiosity or concern, he wasn't sure which—because she'd said she was out of touch with her relatives. Leave it to his mother to do some probing. Sheila was the only Steele who didn't wear a badge, and yet she was just as adept as her sons and husband at getting information from recalcitrant sources. No doubt, as he delved into Judith's background, Nat would discover the reason for the rift with her parents. "Liked them?" Sully echoed. "Meaning?"

"Meaning I hope you're right. I hope there's some reasonable explanation for your father's disappearance."

She was actually being sincere. "You don't look any

more convinced of his innocence than before I took you to the house."

"Maybe not," she murmured. "But it's my job not to be convinced. Anyway, I know looks can be deceiving."

Hers were. Given Judith's trim suits, he'd never have guessed she spent at-home time waltzing across sinfully thick white carpets. "Well...thanks." He knew he should go, but he was suddenly too curious. "Mind if I use the john before I take off?"

Her lips parted, and for a second, Sully was sure she was going to protest, worried about his further surveying her private domain. On the other hand, how could she refuse?

"Sure, Steele." As she tossed her head, thick dark hair swung over her shoulder, chocolate curls licking her bare skin. She nodded, looking uncomfortable. "It's, uh, through the bedroom."

The bedroom. Somehow, he felt like a lucky man. "Thanks."

Leaving the file on a table, he headed in the direction she indicated, listening to her soft footsteps behind him. Pausing before he crossed the threshold, he took a deep breath and then he entered the room where she slept. Her long arm almost grazed his head—he felt the air move—as she reached to flick a switch. Instead of an overhead fixture, softly glowing pink bulbs illuminated the room; they were placed randomly about, creating the effect of candlelight. Her voice caught, sounding anxious. "There. Keep going and you'll hit the bathroom. You'll find a light above the mirror."

"I appreciate it," he managed, unable to lift his gaze from where it landed—on her bed.

"No problem," she said.

But everything in her tone said it was. And he could sure see why. Still sensing her presence behind him, Sully slowly ran his gaze around the room. Here, as in the rest of the apartment, the carpet was white. The sole piece of furniture was a canopied bed in the room's center; its supports were of aluminum, its curtains fashioned from transparent, gossamer silver fabric. Piled high with pillows and covered with a silver duvet, the bed looked more than inviting.

"Steele," Judith said in warning.

What did she think he was going to do? Walk over, draw back the covers and get in? He couldn't help but blow out a low wolf whistle, then chuckle softly. "What?" He tossed the challenge over his shoulder as he headed toward the bathroom. "Are you afraid I'm going to blackmail you?" Definitely, no one in New York law enforcement would guess Judith Hunt had the world's most romantic bedroom.

"Fortunately, I work for Internal Affairs," she retorted. "If you blackmail me, I can prosecute."

"If you're really tough," he countered, feeling her eyes on his back, "maybe you'll add a breaking and entering charge."

"Not to mention public indecency."

Smiling, he couldn't help but say, "Oh, Judith, you have no idea how indecent I can be."

She exhaled a peeved sigh. "I can guess, Steele."

"Good," he shot back lightly, barely able to believe they were actually flirting. He entered the bathroom, and right before he shut the door, he added, "I'll just leave you to your imagination then, Judith."

Meantime, Sully took in a bathroom that was every bit as feminine as the bedroom. His gut tightened as he drew a sharp breath. On the lip of the tub, filled with a spray of wildflowers, was an amber bottle exactly like the one he'd tossed into the Hudson. Sully's first thought was that he'd been corresponding with Judith, but he quickly amended the notion. It was impossible. Too much coincidence. Besides, hadn't the clerk in the shop said such bottles were common?

His eyes trailed past the flowers to a crystal container of bath salts and a cache of floating candles, both of which Sully could only assume Judith used in the tub. The shower curtain was of smoky silver, the towels white, thick and luxurious. One was still damp. Tossed on the lid of a hamper, it smelled of fragrant floral soap. Sully's groin pulled. God, he'd love to see Judith's tall, svelte body naked. Love to watch her drying herself, briskly rubbing a terry towel over long-boned thighs after stepping from the shower...

Dammit, if he didn't quit thinking like this, he was going to wind up in trouble. Distracting himself, he opened the mirrored cabinet and glanced over the neatly arranged toiletries. He had no idea what he expected to find.

"Maybe this," he whispered, turning toward the back of the door. From a hook hung one of the most sinful robes he'd ever seen. Long, white and utterly sheer, it would reveal every inch of a woman's body. Reaching out, he couldn't help but finger the barely there fabric. The next thing he knew, he'd pulled it to his face and drawn in her scent. Heat pooled in his lower belly, and he felt suddenly breathless, as if bands were tightening around his chest. Apparently, prim Judith spent her spare time lounging in a bed made for lovemaking, wearing see-through gowns.

"I'd better get out of here," Sully whispered, giving the toilet an obligatory flush and washing his hands. When he came out, Judith was framed in the doorway of the bedroom, her arms crossed over her chest. Light from the living room was shining behind her, and through her dress, Sully could make out a triangular wedge where her legs met.

"You were snooping," she challenged, looking perturbed.

He lifted his gaze to hers. "What a suspicious mind."

"Steele..." she warned.

"And I thought I'd left you standing there," he said in what was almost a drawl, "thinking about how indecent I could be."

Color rose on her pale cheeks. "The walls are paper thin, and I know you just flushed."

"Excellent detection skills," he complimented.

Her eyes narrowed. "Comes with the job."

"And it makes me glad you work for I.A. As a clean, rather than a dirty cop, I feel so much safer."

"*If* you're a clean cop."

Her blue eyes were piercing through him, and as she tightened her arms in front of her chest, her breasts raised a fraction, as if for his perusal. That hadn't been her intention, of course. Nevertheless...

He swallowed hard. "I—and my precinct—are as clean as a whistle, Judith."

"If not, the whistle will get blown. On you, Steele."

"Thanks for the warning."

"Dinner was good, but I don't want you to get the impression I'll soften up."

"You soften?" He arched a brow. "Never."

"Good. Just so you understand that."

He had the sudden urge to tell her everything about her was sexy—even her damn threats. Another rush of heat slid through his veins. "I don't want you to soften," he added. "I want my father found."

"I always get my man."

"I can think of ten different responses to that."

"But surely there are better uses for such a sharp mind." Imagining seeing her undressed was one. "Surely," he agreed, thinking once more of the transparent bathrobe. Not that she needed to wear it, given how the living room light was shining through her dress. His mouth had turned cottony. He wasn't enough of a gentleman not to look, and every time he did, his heart nearly stopped. He could see the apex of her thighs and the slight parting of her legs.

Oblivious, she said, "Find anything interesting during your investigation of my bathroom, Steele?"

Ignoring the slow, insistent burn of desire, he started across the bedroom, a tempting smile pulling at the corners of his lips. "I may have found a few incriminating things," he admitted.

"I won't ask what. I can guess."

Was it his imagination, or had her breath quickened with his approach? He stopped before her, surprised when she didn't step aside. "Flowers?" he said, his voice turning husky with her close proximity. "Floating candles?"

Tilting her chin, she looked at him from under the heavy lids of her eyes. "I'm not the person you think I am."

His mind was still on the robe. "Obviously not. Where'd you find the amber bottle? The one on the lip of the tub?"

She continued eyeing him. "Why?"

"Just curious."

She considered, then stated calmly, "It was a gift."

"From anybody special?"

"You sound jealous, Steele."

Hell, maybe he was. "Do you know a lot of men?"

"How insulting."

But Judith didn't look insulted, not really. In fact, he could swear she looked a little pleased that he'd asked. Sully forced himself to draw another slow, steady breath. Yes, indeed, he and Judith Hunt were now walking into very dangerous territory. He edged closer, his back gliding along the door frame, so that he shared the threshold with her—Judith leaning on one side of the doorjamb, him on the other. "Sorry," he murmured.

"You should be."

Whatever he did next was crucial. This had the feel of a moment that would end in one of two ways—with him tossed out on the sidewalk or landing in her bed. He let his voice drop, becoming throaty and seductive, since she might as well know what was on his mind. "I'd be jealous of any man who got to see you wearing the robe on the back of the bathroom door."

She stared at him a long moment, her expression unreadable. And then she said, "You liked it?"

He rolled his eyes. "Wouldn't any man?"

"Hey," she chided. "And I thought you were special, Steele."

"Am I?" *To you?* His eyes added the words.

She shrugged. "I'll take the fifth."

At that moment, he damned her voice for being so cool and matter-of-fact. She could have been in court. Challenged, he felt even more compelled to hear her surrender. As Sully moved closer, leaving scant inches between them, he was imagining soft pants and ragged sighs. The breath she drew was neither, but it was audible and exciting, a slight, anticipatory hitch that made his blood dance.

"The fifth?" he murmured in lazy inquiry. "If you're not going to talk, Judith, is there something else you'd rather do?"

"Careful, Steele, you're heading toward obstruction of justice."

"Is that your only charge?"

"I could add sexual harassment."

"Is that what I'm doing with you?" Angling his head down, he brought his lips near enough to hers that he could feel the tantalizing heat of her breath swirl on his cheek. "Being sexual?"

She flattened a hand on his chest, splaying her fingers. Glancing down, he felt another pang of undeniable arousal when he saw the neatly manicured, white-tipped nails digging into his shirt. He decided he needed to see them tangling in his chest hair. Which meant he would. Sullivan Steele always got the things he needed. Or wanted.

"What you're doing, Captain Steele," Judith said pointedly, the glossy awareness in her eyes indicating that she, too, felt the ricocheting body heat, "is going home."

"Captain?" She'd never called him that, he thought, leaning a fraction closer. "Why don't you call me Sully, like everybody else?"

"Maybe I will. If you're good."

"That might be a long wait," he conceded.

"Then Sullivan it is."

Just once, he wanted to hear her call him Sully. It was so much more familiar, and he could easily imagine how it might sound, coming with a high keening cry of female desire.

She jerked her head toward the front door, but otherwise didn't move. "You're wearing out your welcome."

"If you aren't the hostess with the mostest."

"Home," she commanded.

"If you insist." He didn't bother to hide that his breath was becoming labored because she was so close and smelled like heaven. "But I'm not leaving before I tell you..."

She tried to edge away, as if she'd just now guessed what was coming, but with her back pressed against the doorjamb, there was nowhere for her to go. He took advantage, angling into the remaining space until their bodies nearly touched.

"Tell me what?" she asked.

"Tell you that, deep down, you don't really want me to leave."

She scoffed. "I'd arrest you, Steele—" a sudden soft purring of her voice took the sting from the words "—but you don't belong in a jail cell. Now I know you belong in a mental health facility."

He barely heard the words, only registered the telltale catch in her voice. Before he thought it through, the words came out. "You want me to kiss you," he coaxed. When she didn't protest, he leaned down, his lips grazing her cheek, lightly moving toward her mouth.

"Dammit, Steele," she cursed softly. "You know better than this."

"Probably," he murmured. "But you weaken my defenses."

"What do you want from me?" she managed to gasp.

"A lot of things. I'd like to see you in that robe, for instance," he whispered, his body pressing forward, colliding with hers, their bellies gently brushing.

She was trying—and failing—to look as if she didn't like the feel of his hard body against hers. "I wouldn't hold your breath."

"I never do when I kiss a woman."

"You're sure of yourself, Steele."

"I'm sure of you, too."

Her breath sounded uneven now. "What's that supposed to mean?"

It meant he could feel the sexual tension mounting in her body. Inviting warmth was pouring from her despite the air-conditioning, and Sully figured it was only seconds until his hands would be exploring her silken thighs, pushing the fabric of her dress up, so he could cup her mound through her panties. "Quit fighting me, Judith," he said silkily, his lips brushing over hers, ever so lightly.

"Obstruction of justice," she warned, her voice quivering in a way that satisfied him immensely. "And I'm no fool. I know exactly what you're doing."

"Do you?" His words communicated the heat he felt coiling inside him, as did his throaty chuckle. "It's nice to see you're as sharp in the bedroom as in the office."

"You're just trying to get me to go soft on your father," she accused again.

Maybe. But he was also about to show her lovemaking such as she'd never seen before. "Actually, I've got another agenda right now, Judith."

"Cut me some slack, Sully."

"You seem determined to ignore what's happening between us."

"Right. I do. Nothing's happening."

"Oh, really?" Swiftly, he brought his lips directly above hers and let them hover. Hers were glossy and crimson, and he'd never been so hungry to nibble anything. Patiently, he let a second pass during which their eyes locked. A long, tension-filled moment followed.

"Is something happening now?" he challenged softly, and then, before she could answer, his mouth lowered. Slowly, hotly, he took her lips, using his to ease them apart. After a languid moment, he nudged them farther, just enough that his tongue could slide inside.

She was more eager than he'd anticipated. Satisfaction rumbled through him as the interior of her mouth welcomed him, feeling as searing and wet as her lips and as creamy as her lipstick. He groaned deep in his throat when he felt the experimental dart of her tongue, its touch like sun-warmed, damp velvet as it glided over his.

When she flicked it, his arousal was complete. Already, he knew there was no turning back; this kiss was taking them to bed. Hadn't he known she'd draw such a wild response from him? Hadn't he daydreamed of this every time he'd ever seen her in the precinct? Hadn't he fantasized about the time—just moments away now—when they'd both be naked and he'd be stiff and pushing deep inside her?

His lips loosened, slackening on top of hers as he deepened the openmouthed kiss. Thrusting his tongue, he felt her melt with the new assault. Stroke for languid, masterful stroke, she kissed him back, until fire was coursing through his veins, tunneling down into his extremities, making heat flow through him like lava.

Boldly, on a rush of passion, his hands glided up her pink dress until they paused just inches from the outer sides of her breasts. He hesitated, his mouth still locked to hers, and when she didn't protest, he cupped the mounds of flesh, gently molding the contours. He lightly brushed the nipples. Feeling them harden through fabric, he felt a renewed urgency that drove him to break their kiss. On impulse, unable to stop himself, he leaned down and licked her breasts through the dress until the strong strokes of his tongue had liberally wet the silk.

"Judith," he uttered simply, wishing his mouth was fixed to a bare, peaked tip. "I really think we ought to go to bed." Rather than answering, she gasped, and in response, he closed his lips tightly, clamping them over a hot, tight bud. Using his teeth, he scraped where she was so aroused, making her shudder.

"C'mon," he murmured, knowing he couldn't take much more. Lowering his hands to her waist, he pulled her toward the bed, which was tailor-made for romance.

"Dammit, Steele," she muttered shakily. "Like I said, I know exactly what you're doing—" They were nearly on the mattress when she managed to twist away from him.

He grabbed her hand. "You want this every bit as much as I do, Judith." He was unsteady on his feet because of how much he wanted her; he'd fantasized about her for so long.

"No, I don't."

"Liar."

When he swung her nearer, the movement made their hips collide. He was big with need now, thoroughly engorged, his arousal thick and aching—and when she felt him nestling between her legs, she froze. At the startled look in her blue eyes, he felt desire ebb; concern came in its wake. "Judith?" he whispered, squinting. What was happening? It was as if something had frightened her. "Are you okay?"

She regained her composure. "Fine."

"No, you're not," he countered.

"I am."

"You don't look fine." She looked...surprised. Worried. Scared.

"I'm fine," she repeated.

Well, maybe she was. Her body had relaxed. Her eyes fixed on his, and she shook her head as if to clear it. While her words were firm, her voice still held a tremor. "I'll say it one more time, Steele. I'm no fool. You're just trying to get close to me so I'll share information."

"You were already sharing information," he reminded her, tightening the fingers that had threaded through hers. He paused, then decided there was no use lying to her. She was sharp as a tack. "Anyway, maybe that was true before, but now everything's different, Judith...." Now, they were only a foot from her bed.

"You expect me to believe that, Steele?"

"Of course I do."

Her eyes suddenly flashed, turning a deep cobalt-blue in the dim light of the room. "I'm a cop, too. My mind's every bit as devious as yours."

"Exactly," he murmured throatily. Through the wet spots on her dress, he could see every sexy detail. "Your deviousness is one of the things that most excites me."

"You're impossible, Steele."

"And you're wrong about my motives," he replied simply, straining to keep his voice even, despite how deeply she'd excited and unsettled him. He wanted her, he'd wanted her for years, and he was willing to take this wherever it went. Gaining control of himself, he gently added, "Judith...please..."

She tried to step away, but he wasn't about to let her go. Once more he tightened his grip, trailing his fingers over the back of her hand.

"Let me go," she choked out. Her voice was low, raspy. "What do you want from me, Steele?"

Urgently, he drew her flush against him. "You know what I want." His breath turned harsh at the feel of her lower body pressed to his. He stared down, his gaze like a laser. "You. In bed."

She could barely breathe. "Me and the Great Protector, huh?"

"That's right."

"I don't need a man to protect me."

"Maybe that'll free you up, so you can need a man for other things."

"Such as?"

"Shared pleasure."

Her chin was tilted up. She was still pressed against him, and their bodies weren't just hot now, they were burning. Her words were as simple as they were succinct. "We can't do this."

"Maybe not," he conceded. "But we're going to."

"Damn," she cursed softly. It was the only word she managed before Sully's mouth swooped down and captured hers once more.

HE'D SCARED HER. A moment ago, Judith had felt wrenched back in time. She'd had no control when her body reacted. She'd frozen like ice, her mind going blank.

Fortunately, despite his razor-honed instincts, Sullivan hadn't noticed. He'd thought she didn't want to make love because they worked together.

Which we do, she reminded herself as his firm lips moved on hers. Her boss would probably fire her for this. "You have to go, Sullivan," she managed to whisper on a ragged sigh, the words nearly lost against his mouth.

"Sully," he corrected, the tantalizing flick of his tongue sending delicious feelings swirling through her. "You said you'd call me Sully if I was good."

It was wrong, but somehow she couldn't stop her arms from wreathing around his neck. Nobody had ever kissed her like this. Each touch of his mouth was creating waves of internal shivers. For so long, she'd hoped a man would sweep into her life and arouse her in a way she couldn't deny, exactly the way Sullivan Steele was now. "Just kiss me, Steele."

His voice was almost a growl. "What the hell do you think I'm doing?"

"Talking."

"Not anymore."

And he wasn't. He was kissing her deeply again, his hands rising and gently kneading her breasts until the core of her ached so much she whimpered. His hands closed, squeezed, caressed, maddened. She'd never been touched like this; her few experiences with men hadn't been entirely fulfilling, not that she'd tell Sullivan. She schooled herself to breathe slowly, to savor the sensations. Especially how her breasts felt, both hot and cold by turns, since the spots left by his ravenous, practiced mouth were now being cooled by the relatively chill air of the room, then re-heated by his exploring hands.

"C'mon." When he urged her to the bed, she went gladly. A second later, she was lying on her back and he was climbing on top of her. Her breath caught. She expected his weight to be uncomfortable, thought she'd feel crushed and panicky, but every long, muscular inch just felt good. So good that Judith very quickly worked off his shirt.

"Yes," she whispered encouragingly. His chest was hard. Strewn with golden hair. And it was settling against the cushion of her breasts as his mouth angled across hers. Slowly, he was devouring her, making her shake inside. Her dress hem had risen all the way up to her panties. She felt feverish, damp all over. Suddenly, his hand was pressing between her legs. He stroked her inner thighs, too, trailing the backs of his fingers up and down, from her knees to the leg band of her panties.

"Open for me," he coaxed hoarsely.

Spurred by his excited panting, she did as he asked, and now his hand swept to her core again, finding the fabric of her panties as wet as the top of her dress, she was sure. As he inched down, she tried to stop him, tangling her fingers in short hair that looked like spun gold and felt like silk. But it was too late.

She felt his head between her legs, the soft strands of his hair brushing her thighs. And then his mouth settled where she was open. Right through her panties, he kissed her. Deep and wet and hot, his openmouthed ministrations sent burning tingles through her in undulating waves, and she tilted back her head abruptly as the sudden thrust of his tongue met her own wet heat.

Her heart was pounding, beating too hard in her chest, and when he buried his face deeper, she clutched his head wildly and glided her hands over his broad shoulders. He was so strong! So male! With a sudden, harsh catch of breath, she felt him move against her with urgent need.

He was pushing her dress up...up....

His mouth was quickening, his lips pushing against her lower lips, the fabric covering her now so drenched that it was no barrier to the soft seductive movements of his tongue. He circled its pointed tip around the bud. Around and around, until she thought she'd go crazy. Her mind went dark and hazy. All her control was lost. She was gasping and crying out, begging for more. Building heat suddenly made her hips jerk; she arched from the mattress, seeking and straining.

"Loosen up for me," he urged in a moan.

Her body was so tight, she thought vaguely. But she felt so hot...so bothered as he pushed her thighs open wider. Her inner muscles stretched as he slid his hands beneath her, stripped away wet silk and cupped her bare backside. Moaning, she felt his searing mouth settle again—this time on unprotected flesh—and she surged. A sudden thrust of his tongue brought her to the brink of satisfaction.

She hovered there as both his broad, splayed hands slid farther up, under her dress. He caressed her belly before rising briefly to pull the dress over her head, leaving her completely naked. Burning hot, his hands found her breasts. Rougher now, he pinched and twisted the tips, rolled them between his fingers and flicked his thumb mercilessly against the buds.

Judith could barely breathe, and when she did, she could only say his name. "Sullivan."

All movement ceased for a second. "Sully," he corrected. "You said you'd call me Sully if I was good."

And God, was he good!

As if he didn't know it, he prodded. "Am I?"

"Yes...yes..."

"What's my name?"

"Sully," she cried, knowing she'd always think of him that way after this. "Sully!"

She'd never known she could be so open and free with a man. But Sully Steele was so good that she had no choice, no will of her own. Before she knew it her legs were practically wrapped around his head, and writhing, she clutched his hair as luscious spasms claimed her. She let herself go completely, only vaguely aware of the husky panting and deep, breathy sighs breaking the silence.

She was still lost when his mouth slammed into hers again. She could taste him, taste herself, and she'd never imagined a moment—or a kiss—so sexy. Sexier still when she realized his belt was undone, his zipper down, his erection a bold, inviting thrust against her center. Her hands trembling, she helped him push down his slacks and briefs. A condom came from somewhere; Judith didn't know or care where, just so they had it. She panted with need, unable to do anything other than stare as he sheathed himself. He was perfect. Everything a man should be.

"We shouldn't be doing this," she managed to gasp, her senses reemerging for the briefest of seconds. "We work together." And she was out to prosecute his father.

"Why don't we worry about that tomorrow?" Sully said, gliding on top of her once more. Somehow, she'd expected him just to plunge inside her. Instead, he rolled, smoothing his hands over her hips and bringing her on top of him, so her knees bracketed his sides.

"I'm yours now," he whispered, the dark, throaty words full of encouragement. "Do whatever you want...what we both want...."

It was almost as if he knew what she needed. It was her first time in so long, and he was giving her exactly that—the opportunity to take control and set the pace. Quickly, he helped lift her, and as she slowly slid down the length of his hot, engorged shaft, she felt sensations building inside her again, cresting as she took him deeper...and felt him stretching her, filling her....

This wouldn't last long. Before, they'd been running on raw passion, but now, watching how generously Sullivan—Sully, Judith corrected mentally—matched her needs, she felt whatever ice was around her heart slowly start melting.

"Sully," she whispered again.

His face was flushed with desire. He was watching her through beautiful, heavy-lidded amber eyes. His lips were parted, his tongue pressed to the upper one in anticipation of their next kiss. "Yes?" he whispered simply, his eyes traveling over her face.

Her answer was a gasp of satisfaction. His response the tightening of fingers on her hips as he urged her to take them both over the top. Only then did his eyes shut in bliss. And right then, studying his face while her body shared his pleasure, Judith could swear she was falling in love.

5

HAD SHE REALLY—however briefly—thought she could fall in love with Sully Steele? "It's only sex," Judith whispered to herself in reminder. It had been days since they'd first shared a bed, but she knew better than to start trusting Sully. Betrayal, she well knew, often rode on the heels of trust. Just when life was perfect, things could catch you off guard. Take you by surprise. Smart women always braced themselves for it.

She sighed. As a prosecutor employed by the police department, she was far too smart and rational to lose her head over a man, anyway. And besides, she knew what Sully was really after: news about his father. Not that Judith had much to offer. But she had to be careful not to get caught up in the heat of the moment....

Standing before a full-length mirror, she smoothed her hands over her hips, taking in the white sleeveless dress she'd chosen to wear to meet Mr. X. *Perfect*, she thought. The dress was pretty and feminine, but not too suggestive. In this sweltering heat, the light fabric would keep her cool. Outside, the mercury was pushing a hundred, and the humidity had turned the air as thick as molasses. She'd pulled her hair into a French twist to better combat the heat. Hopefully, she wouldn't be in Central Park too long, standing on the bridge overlooking Bethesda Fountain, dripping with sweat and looking frizzy.

Reaching out, she whisked a long, oblong silk scarf from the bed she'd been sharing with Sully. Casually, she looped it around her neck, a slash of red, then arranged the ends so they hung in front of her.

She tried to shrug off guilt when she looked at the side of the bed Sully had claimed as his own. Sure, she was meeting another man this evening, but she and Sully were just having sex, right? And she wasn't going to *sleep* with Mr. X., right? In fact, she'd already decided that, after today, she'd probably never see Mr. X again.

She probably shouldn't see Sully, either. Purely sexual relationships such as theirs were probably a dime a dozen for a man like him, anyway. And if her boss got wind of the affair, he'd read her the riot act. Or worse. Sleeping with one of the Steele brothers wasn't exactly illegal, but in Judith's book, it was pretty damn unethical.

And yet it felt too good to stop. Just thinking about Sully made her knees go weak. Yes, she should have called it quits after that first time, but she'd never imagined sex could get so lusty. With Sully, she was learning to abandon herself. To surrender. To ask for things she wanted. With her, the man was definitely making good on the name he'd earned around the precinct.

"The Protector," she murmured.

She'd never felt as safe as she did with him in bed. A sizzle of warm sensation shot through her now, teasing all her erogenous zones. She shuddered. Pleasure—and steamy memories of it—were with her all the time. By day, when they met, they were strictly professional, of course. But every night...

She blew out a shaky breath. Well, things would be fine as long as she didn't get emotionally involved, right? No doubt Sully was thinking the same thing. It was probably why he hadn't sounded too perturbed when she'd made herself unavailable tonight.

"Lied to him," she whispered in correction, thinking of his call this afternoon. Before he'd had the chance to invite himself over, she'd plunged in. "Sorry to disappoint you, Steele, but we'll have to take a rain check."

While it was hard to admit, Judith wished he'd at least sounded disappointed. "Hot date?" he'd teased.

She shouldn't have said it, but she did. "Careful, or I'll think you sound relieved."

"At missing a night between your sheets?" He'd chuckled softly. "Hardly, Judith."

She'd sucked in a breath. Sully had been tutoring every inch of her, his mouth and hands teaching her new ways to enjoy herself while he showed her how to bring his own body alive.

At first, she'd felt tugs at her heartstrings and a surge of unwanted hope and trust. She'd even imagined her and Sully Steele getting married! How utterly ludicrous! As soon as she'd caught herself fantasizing about walking down the aisle, she'd laughed out loud. No, she would let a man get only so close. Which meant never close enough to burn her. Yes, tonight she was merely putting some very necessary distance between her and Sully....

The man she'd agreed to meet in the park, at least judging from his letters, was a whole other breed. Never pushy, always respectful, he was probably incapable of the duplicity that made her and Sully so good at their jobs. She'd already decided not to pursue the relationship. "But he's safe, stable, reliable," she whispered aloud.

Just as she usually was. Unfortunately, sex with Sully had thrown Judith off her game. She was still trying to get the warrants that would allow her to delve into Sheila Steele's bank records. There were no fresh leads on Augustus, although she'd discovered that the mysterious estate on Seduction Island, Castle O'Lannaise, was owned by Tommy the Jaw, the ex-mobster who'd also owned the *Destiny*, and who had, once-upon-a-time, turned state's evidence for Augustus Steele.

"Yeah. Very neat. The threads of this case are going to unravel soon." She felt a rush of excitement, then another twinge of guilt. Too bad Sully was probably going to get hurt. She didn't want to be there when the glitter dust wore off and he realized the father he'd idolized was nothing more than a common crook.

But then, maybe she was wrong.

She cursed softly. Yes, there it was again: this renewed desire to trust human nature! If she wasn't careful, Sully was going to turn her to mush, and in her line of work, that could get her killed. Or at least fired.

Maybe Sully already knows his father's guilty. She pushed aside the errant thought. "Get out of here, Judith," she muttered. "You're going to be late." Lifting her keys from the bed, she slipped them into a tiny red shoulder bag. While it was open, she withdrew a tube of crimson lipstick. After she'd coated her lips, she slipped into red high heels and slid on sunglasses. She hoped she didn't have to wait long for a cab. Why hadn't she suggested she meet her pen pal somewhere air-conditioned?

"At least you decided to meet him."

It was the right thing to do. At this point it was too late to cancel. "Maybe tonight'll take the edge off," she muttered. And maybe, just maybe, her deepest suspicions were wrong—and Sully Steele's father was innocent.

I'M TOO OLD for this kind of action. That was the thought in Augustus's mind as the crowded ferry approached Manhattan. He glanced behind him, over the heads of tourists and commuters, at the Statue of Liberty and Ellis Island, then returned his gaze to the skyline, squinting where brilliant white sunlight ricocheted from shiny steel skyscrapers. Augustus shook his head. What the hell had he done? Retirement had been right around the corner. All he'd had to do was sit tight. Yes, he was far too old to be having these high-stakes adventures.

He barely felt the breeze buffeting his face, and despite the danger of carrying so much money, he hardly registered the heaviness of the suitcases he was holding. Maybe his boy Rex was right when he said his pop always thought of himself first, not the family. Rex had said Augustus only lived for the adrenaline rush and high-stakes gambles that came with carrying a badge and a gun.

Trying not to dwell on the retirement plans he'd made with Sheila, Augustus focused his attention on the choppy waters lapping the ferry's hull. Hell, if fate was with him, and if everything went right, he and Sheila would be even better able to enjoy their golden years....

He gripped the suitcase handles more tightly. It was a good thing no one could guess that money was inside—or how much. All Augustus needed was some hotshot kid from Brooklyn or the Bronx grabbing one of the cases, thinking that Augustus—like many other people on the ferry—was a tourist who might be carrying something worth stealing.

Seven million dollars, of course, was pretty well worth stealing. The inner workings of the boat groaned as the hull came dockside, and Augustus took a deep breath. Maybe he should have stayed on Seduction Island. Weeks ago, when the *Destiny* exploded, he'd barely made it ashore with all the cash. Something had happened; at first, feeling disoriented, he'd thought amoebas in the ocean water had made him sick. Then he'd remembered that the other man on the boat had poisoned him. For weeks he'd been laid up and recovering, hiding in the attic of Castle O'Lannaise, the big estate owned by Tommy the Jaw.

Augustus had hoped to stay there. But then somebody—maybe an undercover cop, possibly one of Joe Gregory's guys—had started going over Castle O'Lannaise with a fine-tooth comb. Fearing he was getting too close, Augustus had fled Seduction Island.

Now he listened as an outside ferry ramp clanked into place. When the crowd began moving toward the exit, he felt himself swept along. He took a deep breath as he stepped onto the land.

Augustus Steele—and the seven million dollars he'd stolen—were back on Manhattan Island again.

AT THE EXACT SAME MOMENT, Sully was starting up the staircase to the bridge that overlooked Bethesda Fountain in Central Park. Suddenly, he stopped in his tracks and stared. Cabs had been scarce and he was ten minutes late; he'd been moving fast through an unbearable heat wave, dodging the crowd as he slipped out of a sports coat, which he held over his shoulder by the hook of a finger. Now he considered his next move.

Oh, for a second, he was surprised to see Judith. But then he registered the red scarf, remembered the amber bottle on the lip of her tub and realized she—of all people—really was the mystery woman he'd come here to meet.

Sully was nothing if not flexible. Years on the force had taught him to gauge situations and make shifts in plans. "Only in New York," he muttered, rifling a hand through hair that, given the temperature, was thankfully short.

How, in a city of seven million, had it turned out that Judith had found the bottle he'd tossed into the Hudson? And yet it made sense. Whenever she didn't drive to the precinct, she'd walk up to Hudson Street, where it was easier to catch a cab. Apparently, she'd taken walks along his favorite pier. Staring up at her,

Sully cursed under his breath. No doubt the bottle had washed back to shore....

"Lady of my dreams," he muttered softly, and then recalled one of her last letters. "I haven't dated anyone in a long time, and I'm not sure what I'm really looking for. Casual dating? A steady companion? Marriage? Like I said, I'm just not sure, Mr. X. I hope you're not turned off by my confusion...."

"Casual dating? Marriage?" Sully punctuated the words with a softly spoken oath. "What about unbridled sex?" Why hadn't Judith bothered to mention that as an option? It was what she'd been doing with *him*, after all. And it grated. Now that he thought about it, in bed she really *hadn't* talked to him as intimately as she did in her letters to "Mr. X."

Sully knitted his eyebrows. He and Judith hadn't yet gone out. No dinner, no movies. Every night, she insisted on going straight to bed. Not that Sully had minded...

At least not until now. But here she was, dressed to kill and meeting a man with whom she'd been busy sharing her innermost thoughts. Yeah, Judith was definitely more devious than he'd imagined. In addition to cultivating two men at once—one for the heart and one for her pleasure—she was holding her own as Joe Gregory's top dog down at Police Plaza.

"I can't believe this," Sully muttered, tamping down a rush of emotion—which, under the circumstances, was ridiculous. "Am I really jealous of myself?" He was tempted to stride straight up the stairs and confront her.

"Working late tonight?" he might say.

Of course, when he'd called her earlier, he'd been about to make the same excuse. And to think he'd felt less guilty when Judith had beaten him to the punch....

His groin tightened as he took her in. *Gorgeous* was the first word that came to mind. She'd rested her smooth bare elbows on the stone railing, and lower, through stone banisters, he caught glimpses of the white dress she wore. A slight August breeze kept lifting the hem, making it sweep across her bare knees. He took in the jewel neck, then the slivers of red where the tails of a silk scarf fluttered against white fabric. Small round sunglasses of the sort associated with John Lennon barely covered her eyes, and her dark hair was drawn tightly back in deference to the heat. Late afternoon sunlight slanted in her direction, accentuating the incredible shape of her face—the pale perfect oval and high, sculpted cheekbones.

Suddenly, he longed to remove her glasses and run his thumbs in the hollows beneath her eyes. He wanted to feel the ticklish brush of her eyelashes on his fingertips, and to pull the pins from her hair, one by one.

He wasn't really falling for her, of course. He was just interested in getting information. And in sharing her bed. And yet he knew better. Her bare skin was like silk to the touch, and every minute Sully wasn't with her, he caught himself thinking about her.

This was his favorite spot in Central Park, and his eyes still hadn't moved from where Judith stood above him, taking in the scene—Bethesda Fountain, the boathouse, the ducks gliding on the lake. To her left was Strawberry Field, and behind her, a tree-lined mall overhung with foliage and lined with wrought-iron benches and lamps.

He shook his head. "So this is how she dresses for Mr. X.," he murmured. Last night, Judith had met *him* at the door in the same lackluster gray suit she'd worn to the office. Not that she'd kept it on long...

And not that he had any right to fault her outfit, he reminded himself, glancing down. He had worn a pleated, button-down Panama shirt, tucked into well-tailored tan slacks of loosely woven linen. And he'd brought a dinner jacket. But he really wasn't here for a date. By the time he'd realized Judith was commanding all his attention, and that he no longer wanted to meet the woman he'd been writing to, it was simply too late to cancel.

But why was Judith here? What was going through her mind?

He seriously considered leaving.

Curiosity got the better of him, though, and he tried not to remind himself that curiosity was what killed the cat. He started ascending the staircase. Due to the heat wave, things had been hectic around the precinct, but Nat had started creating a file on Judith. In fact, earlier, while Sully talked with her on the phone, he'd been peering down at a picture from one of her high school yearbooks.

"Hinky," Nat had said, using his favorite word for off-kilter.

Sully had raised an eyebrow as Nat delivered the books. "Huh?"

"The books go to junior year, then stop. Judith wasn't enrolled as a senior."

"Did her folks move?" She'd mentioned Oklahoma, but that didn't mean it was the only place she'd ever lived.

Nat had shaken his head. "Her dad's dead. Cancer when she was three. She probably doesn't remember him much. Her mother remarried when Judith was fourteen."

At fourteen, she had been as beautiful as she was today. A smile lifted the corners of Sully's mouth. From what he'd seen of her school pictures, she'd probably turned the head of every single male in the farming community where she was raised. But had the loss of her father contributed to her independence and defensive streak?

And where had she gone during her senior year? Sully's mind raced as he approached her. Had there been trouble at home? Or had she taken off to live with a boyfriend? With looks like hers, she'd probably had plenty, not that she'd talked about that much.

Suddenly, her chin lifted as if she'd caught his scent on the air. She turned abruptly—and he couldn't help but feel some satisfaction at seeing the shock on her face.

"Hello," he said mildly.

He watched the soft parting of her crimson lips—and Sully enjoyed that, too. He enjoyed knowing he could step up to her and take those lips with his own. Maybe they hadn't yet had a formal date, but he knew he had a claim to her.

Her voice caught. "Sully? What are you doing here?"

Hearing the feigned innocence in her tone, his humor faded. He fought the urge to blow her cover and ask why she was out here, meeting another man. Didn't she like what had been happening between them? He parted his lips to speak, but then remained silent. Sully liked playing his cards close to the vest.

"I'm just taking a stroll." He lifted an eyebrow. "You?"

"The same," she said without missing a beat.

"Nice clothes for a stroll."

"You, too, Steele."

He watched as she surreptitiously glanced down at the delicate silver watch encircling her wrist, and realized she was deciding she'd been stood up. "About ready for some air-conditioning?" he asked, his gaze sweeping over her appreciatively.

She glanced around, obviously torn and wondering whether Mr. X. was here, somewhere, maybe watching her. "What did you have in mind?"

"Dinner." Despite his pique, Sully shot her a smile. "Maybe even a movie."

She squinted, looking at him as if he'd lost his mind. "You mean, like, a date? With you?"

"Not *like* a date," he corrected, his voice so low and husky they could have been in her bedroom. "A date."

"Thanks for clarifying that."

"Objections, Counselor?"

She glanced swiftly around the park once more, and then, probably realizing Mr. X wasn't going to show, nodded decisively. "None. You said the place where you're taking me is cooler, right, Steele?"

"Hell would be cooler than Central Park is right now."

Her lips curled upward as she chuckled. "In that case, it's too bad hell isn't a restaurant."

"Hungry?"

"Starved, Steele." She eyed him suspiciously. "And not for what you're thinking. I want real food tonight."

He pointed one index finger and rubbed his other one over it. "Shame on you for distrusting my motives. If the lady wants real food—" he draped an arm across her shoulders "—I know just the place...."

"COOLER NOW?" Sully murmured two hours later, ever so slowly rubbing a melting ice cube along the inside of her calf.

"Stop that," she groaned as he continued making long, looping circles on her bare skin. "Somebody'll come in and catch us."

"Not a chance." Because the Steeles were friends of Jen Pang, the restaurant owner, Sully had gotten a private room usually reserved for intimate parties. "We're very alone in here. I made sure of that, Judith."

"I'm still eating," she protested.

"Hurry up and finish," he suggested mildly.

"Anybody ever tell you that you're a lousy date?" she grumbled good-naturedly as he glanced over the leftovers from their dinner of Asian delicacies, then watched her lick cream pudding from a dessert spoon. When she was done, she eased away from his ministrations with the ice cube and tucked her legs beneath her, so she could better curl on one of the many plush pillows surrounding the foot-high table. It was designed so diners could sit on the floor, as if the restaurant were Japanese, not Chinese. In keeping with the concept, their shoes had been neatly placed beside the door.

"You're no fun," Sully complained, momentarily giving up and dunking the ice cube into a water glass again.

"What did you do to rate this room, anyway?" She shot him a suspicious glance—and melted when he looked at her, his eyes the same hot amber color of the double whiskey on the rocks he held in his hand. With his eyes heavy-lidded and half-closed, he looked so sexy that they could have been in the middle of making love. "Just like your suit, this dinner must cost a fortune. Aren't you worried that an I.A officer might get suspicious?"

"I'd love to have you interrogate me," he said.

"Tie you up?" She lifted an eyebrow, unable to believe she was flirting like this. "Blindfold you?"

He shrugged. "Actually," he said, switching the subject, "if you're really interested in how I got the room... When Pop and your boss, Joe Gregory, were down here in Chinatown, working gang-related crimes—"

"Right," she murmured. "I'd forgotten Joe worked here."

"Yeah. Well, Jen Pang and Pop got to be friends. And one night, some members of the Dragons of

Play the
LUCKY
Carnival Wheel
Game...

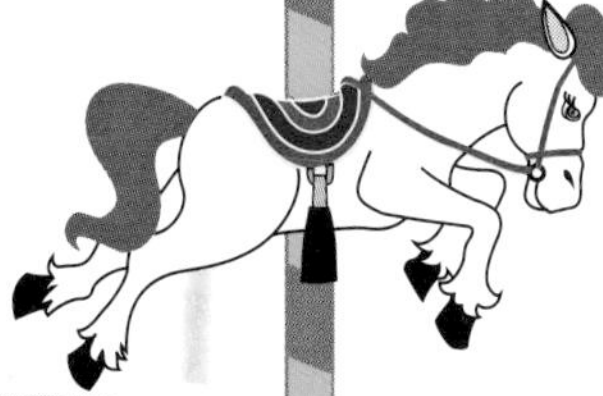

GET YOUR
3 GIFTS
FREE !

PLAY FOR
FREE !
NO PURCHASE
NECESSARY !

HOW TO PLAY:

1. With a coin, carefully scratch off the 3 gold areas on your Lucky Carnival Wheel. By doing so you have qualified to receive everything revealed—2 FREE books and a surprise gift—ABSOLUTELY FREE!
2. Send back this card and you'll receive 2 brand-new Harlequin Temptation® novels. These books have a cover price of $4.25 each in the U.S. and $4.99 each in Canada, but they are yours ABSOLUTELY FREE.
3. There's no catch! You're under no obligation to buy anything. We charge nothing—ZERO—for your first shipment. And you don't have to make any minimum number of purchases—not even one!
4. The fact is thousands of readers enjoy receiving books by mail from the Harlequin Reader Service®. They enjoy the convenience of home delivery...they like getting the best new novels at discount prices, BEFORE they're available in stores... and they love their *Heart to Heart* subscriber newsletter featuring author news, horoscopes, recipes, book reviews and much more!
5. We hope that after receiving your free books you'll want to remain a subscriber. But the choice is yours—to continue or cancel, any time at all! So why not take us up on our invitation, with no risk of any kind. You'll be glad you did!

A surprise gift

FREE

We can't tell you what it is...but we're sure you'll like it! A

FREE GIFT!

just for playing LUCKY CARNIVAL WHEEL!

LUCKY Find Out Instantly The Gifts You Get Absolutely FREE!

Carnival Wheel

Scratch-off Game

Scratch off ALL 3 Gold areas

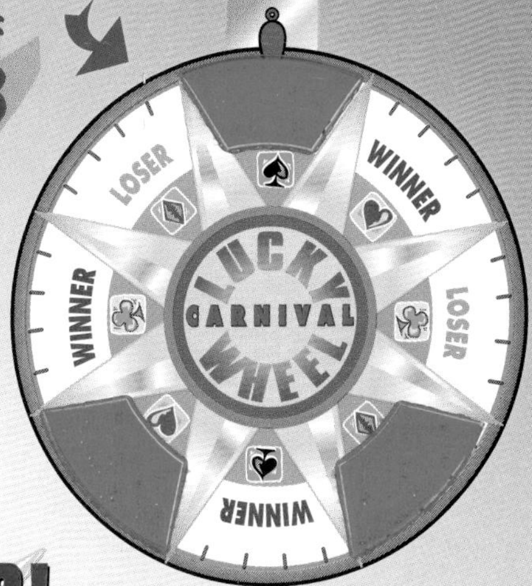

YES! I have scratched off the 3 Gold Areas above. Please send me the 2 FREE books and gift for which I qualify! I understand I am under no obligation to purchase any books, as explained on the back and on the opposite page.

342 HDL DNWX 142 HDL DNWN

FIRST NAME LAST NAME

ADDRESS

APT.# CITY

STATE/PROV. ZIP/POSTAL CODE

Offer limited to one per household and not valid to current Harlequin Temptation® subscribers. All orders subject to approval.

(H-T-08/02)

© 2002 HARLEQUIN ENTERPRISES LTD.
® and ™ are trademarks owned by Harlequin Enterprises Ltd.

The Harlequin Reader Service® —Here's how it works:

Accepting your 2 free books and gift places you under no obligation to buy anything. You may keep the books and gift and return the shipping statement marked "cancel." If you do not cancel, about a month later we'll send you 4 additional novels and bill you just $3.57 each in the U.S., or $4.20 each in Canada, plus 25¢ shipping & handling per book and applicable taxes if any.* That's the complete price and — compared to cover prices of $4.25 each in the U.S. and $4.99 each in Canada—it's quite a bargain! You may cancel at any time, but if you choose to continue, every month we'll send you 4 more books, which you may either purchase at the discount price or return to us and cancel your subscription.

*Terms and prices subject to change without notice. Sales tax applicable in N.Y. Canadian residents will be charged applicable provincial taxes and GST.

If offer card is missing write to: Harlequin Reader Service, 3010 Walden Ave., P.O. Box 1867, Buffalo, NY 14240-1867

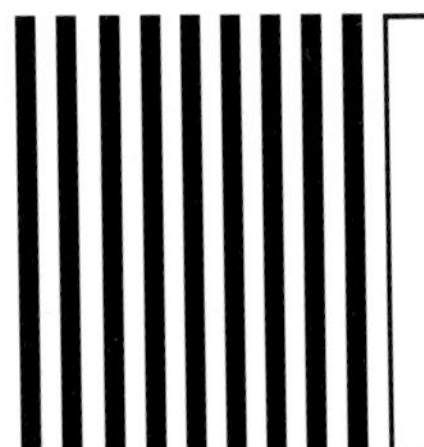

BUSINESS REPLY MAIL

FIRST-CLASS MAIL PERMIT NO. 717-003 BUFFALO, NY

POSTAGE WILL BE PAID BY ADDRESSEE

HARLEQUIN READER SERVICE
3010 WALDEN AVE
PO BOX 1867
BUFFALO NY 14240-9952

Death—a gang that was extorting protection money from business owners on the street—drove by and sprayed bullets through the front window. Pop grabbed Jen's wife and saved her. He was on the cover of the *New York News.* He got a promotion out of it, too. Anyway, my family and the Pangs have continued to be friends. We Steeles have spent Chinese New Year here ever since I can remember."

Judith took a deep breath. Registering the pride in Sully's voice, she really did hope she was wrong about Augustus Steele. Her lips parted, and for a second, she hesitated to speak. "You know that big estate I was telling you about on Seduction Island?" she suddenly said.

Sully raised an eyebrow. "Castle O'Lannaise?"

She nodded. "It turns out my gut instinct was right. It's owned by Tommy the Jaw. I've got an APB out on him, to bring him in for questioning. He owned the *Destiny,* too. If anybody's got information on your father, it'll be him."

"How long have you known that?"

She guessed she didn't blame him for the hint of accusation in his tone. "I don't have to tell you anything, Steele. You know that."

When Sully glanced away, she tried to read the warring emotions in his expression. He looked thoughtful—but she could swear he was also hiding something. She said, "Do you have anything to tell me in return?"

He raised his gaze to hers, and his lips curled in a slow smile. "Tons. But nothing about Pop."

She wanted to probe, but she knew Sully well

enough to know it was useless, especially right now. The eyes drifting over her dress were warm, sparking with male awareness. Desire glinted in those amber orbs just the way the room's dim, romantic light caught in the ice cubes in Sully's whiskey. "Maybe we'd better head back to my place," she murmured huskily.

He tilted the goblet in his hand, took a sip and savored it. She watched as he lifted his fingers to his lips and took an ice cube from between them. "*I'm* not leaving until I interrogate *you*," he murmured, his teasing, playful smile filling her with anticipation.

This time she wasn't going to bother fighting him. "Really?" she asked, moving closer, returning his smile. She hadn't fully understood how much she was growing to like Sully Steele until earlier, when she'd run into him in Central Park. Staring down at the Bethesda Fountain, she'd realized that, if she was honest, she half dreaded meeting the man with whom she'd been corresponding. He was a stranger, after all. And while his letters made him sound safe, what kind of man tossed bottles into the Hudson? Didn't normal men simply go for what they wanted?

Right now, Sully was definitely going for what he wanted.

Judith gasped when she felt the ice trailing up her calf again. This time it wasn't just cold. The cube was hot, too—warmed by whiskey and Sully's mouth. The same mouth he now moved closer and used to cover hers.

"Now," he coaxed between kisses, "what were you

really doing in Central Park, wearing that fancy dress?"

Abruptly, she drew back, her heart missing a beat. For a second, she couldn't move. His question hadn't bothered her. But she hated the taste of alcohol on a man's breath. And yet... Before he could ask her what was wrong, she brought her lips to his again. Maybe the taste wasn't that bad, really. No...it didn't bother her as it used to, she decided. In fact, the whiskey tasted...soothing. Warm. Tangy.

He leaned away as if he meant to withhold satisfaction until he got some answers. "C'mon. What were you doing in Central Park?"

She squinted. "Oh. You're thinking I was meeting a contact. Maybe getting some information."

"I never assume," he corrected. "I'm asking."

She couldn't think of a good reason not to confess, so she told him about finding the bottle in the Hudson. "So," she finished, "I went there to meet him."

Eyes darkened with lust burned into hers. "But you left the park with me. Did you change your mind?"

"He didn't show."

"Disappointed?"

She shook her head. "No," she said honestly. "I'm glad I found you, instead. I...got a lot out of corresponding with him. Like I said, he seemed nice, but when I got there, I had second thoughts about meeting a stranger. And anyway..."

She could swear she heard Sully's breath catch. "Anyway?"

She could scarcely believe she was having this conversation with a man who, around the office, had driven her so crazy. And why did this simple, inconsequential admission of being attracted to him feel so risky? she wondered with a sharp intake of breath. "Anyway," she forced herself to continue, "I...would rather be here with you."

"Glad to hear it."

"Let's get out of here," she whispered against his mouth.

"Let's not."

His tongue darted between her lips, and her legs parted as he brought the ice cube higher on her thigh. She scooted nearer, the hem of her dress catching on a pillow. As the fabric slid higher, Sully's hand followed. Sensations buffeted her—ice melting into her navel, cold water dripping and dampening the silk of her panties, Sully's large warm hand covering the ice, so that both hand and ice were gliding down to slip under the waistband.

"Touch me, Judith," he suggested hoarsely, urging her back on a bed of pillows and coming to lie beside her. Her heart was beating wildly and her body felt oddly out of sync with that. Her limbs felt languid and relaxed, almost drugged—even when she felt the melting ice and his fingers tangling in curls that were already moist. "No," she whispered, "you touch me."

"What say we touch each other?"

"Fair enough, Steele." She reached for him. Already, he was hard. Hard enough that he was straining his zipper, pulling his slacks taut. All it took was a teasing glance to make them both so ready....

Feeling him throbbing through his slacks increased her own excitement, and she opened more for him.

More still, when she heard the soft, needy moan he released while she worked down his zipper.

"Sully Steele," she chided shakily, realizing he'd worn nothing underneath.

"Too hot for anything but slacks," he muttered, the words ragged. His hand was rubbing circles on her sex and his back was arching as she began to touch him the way he'd shown her—with her fingers encircling his length and moving gently, lightly at first....

Vaguely, she wondered how something so cold as the ice could make her so hot. By the time the cube had melted to a sliver, she was shaking, burning up with fever—and just as determined to give him the same kind of pleasure.

"Lie back," she whispered, her insides feeling turbulent as she pushed at his shoulders. She gazed into eyes that had gone smoky, then bent to kiss a mouth slackened by lust. Her heart hammering, she tried senselessly to catch her breath as she shifted her gaze to the intimate part of him. His body was incredible. His slacks were pushed down now, exposing him fully, and desire claimed her. Sharp and quick, it was like nothing she'd ever felt as her eyes followed the upward thrust of his sex. Her gaze settled where he pushed, potent and male, from a riot of tousled golden curls.

Slowly, torturously, feeling her own need soar toward completion as she worked, she massaged her thumbs deep into the hollows of his groin, and then just to tease him, she ceased and ran her hands up and down his bare thighs.

He arched, straining, wanting more. "Please," he

whispered, his voice raspy and fractured. "Please, Judith."

Her own voice was raspy as she murmured, "I never thought I'd hear you beg, Steele."

"Don't tease," he uttered in warning.

"What'll you do to me?" she challenged mildly, loving how aroused he was getting, how much he wanted her. He was too far gone to speak when her hands found him again. A low guttural growl was torn from his throat as she stroked him, eliciting shivers with the flick of her wrist and the playfulness of her fingers. An expectant groan was drawn from him as her grip tightened, a gasp of need as his restless hips involuntarily lifted. With obvious enjoyment he brought his hands upward and clasped them behind his head, his lips parted in ecstasy.

"No," he suddenly said, his eyes flying open at the feel of her tongue.

"Yes," she countered simply, using the point of her tongue to draw dizzy circles around the velvet tip of his sex. The she bent lower to give him the sweet heat of her mouth. His breath hitched while her quickening fingers moved. He reared up. Suddenly, reflexively, he shifted—and before she knew what was happening, he'd reversed their positions.

Now he was on top. It had happened so quickly! Her dress was pushed up, her panties down. At some other time, the dark greed in his eyes might have frightened her or curbed her pleasure, but now it only enhanced it, especially when she felt him settle insistently between her legs. Hard, and impossibly deep, his first thrust was thoroughly unexpected...and so unbelievably good!

"So good," she whispered hazily.

"And about to get better," he whispered back, his words as fractured as her thoughts, which were breaking apart into dark fragments. His mouth angled across hers, quivering with passion. He was still kissing her, wetly and with abandon, when his hands found her hips. He urged her toward him...onto him...around him.

His scent filled her lungs as he plunged even deeper, filling her completely. Crying out, she felt she couldn't take any more. But Sully wasn't done yet. There was so much of him. He was still stretching her.

As he touched her womb, her heart soared. And then, for what promised to become countless hours of bliss, Sully masterfully began to torment her....

6

"STEELE?" Judith murmured in surprise the next day when he knocked on her office door. Her chin abruptly lifted from a stack of papers on her desk, and she stared at him over the rims of rectangular-framed black reading glasses he'd never seen her wear before. Her eyes narrowed, and he could tell she was trying not to react. "Steele," she said again. "I thought we agreed you wouldn't come to my office. What brings you downtown?"

"Nice to see you, too."

"It's *not* nice to see you," she retorted. "We could get in trouble for this."

As Sully swept inside, tossing a navy sport coat to a chair and shutting the door, he could see Judith truly wasn't happy about his visit. Well, he hadn't expected her to be. Just as he hadn't expected to be told she'd requested paperwork allowing her to dig into his personal bank account.

He stared at her a long, murderous moment, barely registering the view through the slats of a window blind behind her: a courtyard separating the countless brick buildings comprising Police Plaza, a glimpse of the white stone mayor's office and a sliver of the Brooklyn Bridge. He glanced around her office, taking in the neatly arranged shelves of leather-bound legal books and file cabinets.

Just as in Judith's apartment, there was nothing extraneous in the office, nothing too telling. Sure, the apartment was luxurious, but it was also empty. No knickknacks, no frills. Judith was the only person Sully had ever met who had nothing but a bed in her bedroom. No, this wasn't the first time he'd begun to think she was hiding something. Nat was still digging into her past, of course, and it was he who'd taken the call from Sully's buddy, Dave Durant, in the warrants department. Dave was better known as Brave Dave, due to the fact that a few years ago, while working the beat as a street cop in Sully's precinct, he'd had a bullet clip his forehead during a bust. The incident had prompted Brave Dave to take a desk job downtown.

"You want me to hold the paperwork, Steele?" Brave Dave had asked when he'd called. "Or let it go through?"

Figuring he had nothing to hide, Sully said, "Let it go through."

"What's she digging into your account for? Somehow, I don't think this has to do with your old man." Brave Dave had chuckled. "Sorry, but rumors fly fast. "Eddie—you know, the redheaded guy down in the criminal records department? He said he saw you and Lips last night, dressed to the nines and going into Jen Pang's in Chinatown for dinner. I said that's crazy. Sully and Lips have been like oil and water ever since she first hit Manhattan. But now...well, I've heard of women hiring P.I.'s to check out the finances of prospective husbands. I guess this is what happens when a man dates a prosecutor from Internal Affairs, right?"

"Long story," Sully had replied, hardly in the mood to kiss and tell. "Maybe another time, Dave."

"Looking forward to it," said Brave Dave. "I'm always available to hear the inside scoop on Lips. Meantime, I'll let the paperwork go through, if that's really what you want, Sully."

"I'm clean as a whistle."

"So's your old man," Brave Dave said before hanging up, "no matter what Lips says. I hear Joe Gregory's hot to arrest him, which sucks, since they used to be partners. Talk about a turncoat. But everybody knows Augustus is a good cop. You Steeles have made more collars than a tailor. Chinatown wouldn't be what it is today without your old man. Anyway, I owe you one, Sully."

It just so happened that Sully had been the first officer on the scene when Brave Dave had gotten shot, so he'd largely been credited with saving the man's life. Even though Sully had gotten a commendation for bravery, he didn't really believe his own good press. Emergency medical technicians, he figured, were due the credit, since they'd gotten Brave Dave to the hospital in record time.

But did Judith really think she was the only one around Manhattan who had contacts? Brave Dave was right. Augustus had been in law enforcement his entire career, and both Sully's brothers were cops. Together, the Steeles were owed more favors than you'd get at a party at the Plaza Hotel.

Judith was eyeing him now, starting to look nervous. "Shouldn't you be in the Village? At the precinct?"

He leaned against the closed door with a casualness he didn't really feel, almost enjoying the slow burn of passionate emotion moving through him. He fought the sudden impulse to pull Judith atop the shiny surface of her desk and—

"We may not have offices this fancy," he said, cutting off his own thoughts and glancing around again as he pushed his hands deep into the pockets of his navy slacks, "but the city's nice enough to give guys like me a lunch break."

She rolled her eyes. "Poor, pitiful you," she chided. "I don't see your brown paper bag, Steele."

"Guess I'm not as hungry as usual."

Apparently getting over her shock at seeing him, she rose and circled the desk. "I guess you'd like to share the reason why you've chosen to forgo your lunch?"

"Like I always say, that's what I like about you. You're quick on the uptake, Judith."

"Well, something must have happened. You've definitely changed your tune since last night."

She *would* remind him of how shamelessly they'd gone at it on the floor of Jen Pang's. After that, Sully had hauled her onto his lap during the cab ride to her place, kissing her senseless and rekindling the heat between them. They'd gone straight to her bed, walking out of their shoes and tumbling onto the mattress. By then, her beautiful white dress was nearly destroyed. He'd tossed it to the floor, badly crumpled. Wrestling with him, she'd broken free and run to the bathroom, and when she'd come out again, she'd been wearing the transparent robe....

Sully swallowed hard now, fighting the swift, aching pull at his groin. As usual, his arousal was fast and complete. All he had to do was look at this woman and he was a goner. As Judith settled her backside against a cherry desk that gleamed to perfection, Sully ignored how traitorously his heart softened at the sight of her. Yeah, he thought dryly, as his gaze drifted down her long legs. Every time he saw her, his heart went softer and his body got harder.

"Go figure," he muttered under his breath.

"Excuse me?"

He sighed wistfully. "Nothing."

She'd left her jacket slung around the back of her chair, and while her gray lawyer's skirt and matching blouse were simple, Judith definitely did the clothes justice. The linen was tasteful, the suit's cut classic. In a court of law, she would set just the right tone: beautiful, but intent on not making use of her female gifts to get ahead in a man's world. Yes, Judith was the type to command respect for her other countless virtues, especially her brains, and until Sully had found out she had a warrant out on him, he'd liked that quality. Now, he wasn't so sure.

She raised a dark, perfectly arched eyebrow. "What are you doing down here, Steele?" She crossed her arms over her chest in a way that, at the moment, struck him as annoyingly imperious. "Did Joe see you? Did you go past his office? You can't come down here on our lunch hour to—"

"You think I came to seduce you?"

Her gaze faltered. "Didn't you?"

"Nice to see you're disappointed."

So she thought he'd come simply for sex. Tempting, Sully admitted, as he pushed himself away from the door with a shoulder and strode toward her. Before she could move, he'd sandwiched her between his body and the desk. "Is that what you were hoping, Judith?" Leaning down, he nuzzled her cheek despite the fury he was trying so hard to keep in check. "That I came downtown just to spice up your day?"

"I'm at work, Steele!"

Powerless to stop himself, he pressed his weight closer, so she could feel the wall of his chest, and lower down, his hard heat. "Thought you'd decided to call me Sully."

"Sully," she muttered. "Steele. Whatever I call you, it won't change the fact that the door doesn't lock."

"Too bad," he murmured, then felt like kicking himself. He'd come down here to confront her, but with her this close, his heart was lurching. The temperature outside was still soaring, and due to the city's latest edict, the air-conditioning in public buildings was still running low to avoid brownouts. That meant the air in the office was musty and close. It should have been unpleasant; instead, it just made him more aware of her scent. Soft floral perfume cut through the humid August warmth, spiraling to his lungs every time he breathed.

Yes, every time he inhaled, he realized she was right. He did want to seduce her. Badly. He was known for patience and perseverance. In the old days, he could last longer than any other officer on a stakeout, but when it came to Judith, all that legendary patience fled. He wanted her. Now. He was almost starting to wish he'd never touched her, never tasted her. She was filling his mind, distracting him from his own cases and from finding his father. He was staying so hot for her that his fingers always itched to touch, while his mouth watered....

He leaned back a fraction, just enough that he could look into her eyes again. "That's what you're doing, isn't it?" he challenged hoarsely. "Distracting me, so you can find Pop before I can."

"You really think I'm that calculating, Steele?"

He hated that she was calling him Steele again. Now, she'd taken to doing that only when he annoyed her. "Yes."

"You know I'm not."

Swallowing hard, he settled a hand on her hip, then glided it downward. Licking his dry lips, he molded his fingers over the smooth linen of the skirt, tracing the curve of her hip. As he did so, he was remembering how she felt underneath that fabric. Her skin was like every sizzling soft thing that melted in a man's mouth; every inch of her was like hot, flaming ice cream or pan-fried butter.

"Last night, you looked so good in that robe," he couldn't help but murmur. It was the last thing he'd meant to say, but with her this close, his lips just inches away from that crimson mouth...

Leaning closer, he brushed his mouth to hers. Against his chest, he felt her firm, high breasts; only when the urge to cup them and roll the taut nipples between his fingers became too much did he lean away.

"We discussed this, remember?" Her lips were pursed, and while there were lights of awareness sparking in her blue eyes, her predominant emotion was pique. "Joe can't see you down here," she said softly, insistently. "What are you thinking, Steele? Are you trying to get me fired?"

Somehow, that grated. "Is that all you care about?" he uttered softly, freeing a hand and dragging it through his hair.

"Yeah. I care about my job. Don't you?"

He'd come here with an agenda, but now he couldn't focus on it. The silken strands of her dark hair were curling on her shoulders, begging for his touch. Her mouth was inviting and gloriously red, as if she'd drunk too much wine. Or as if he'd already been kissing her for hours. Suddenly, he wanted to kiss off all her lipstick...wanted to kiss her until her mouth looked like this naturally—swollen and red. And those eyes! Damn those eyes that were flashing blue fire at him!

She was staring at him, astonished. "Sully, are you even listening to me? This is my career."

"And I'll bet that's more important to you than anything," he muttered, hating himself for it, but wanting to ignite her passion. His eyes drifted over her sculpted face, so slowly that he could have been looking at her for the very first time. She was probably the most ambitious woman he'd ever known, and while he respected that, he wanted what was happening between them to matter more than a career.

"I worked hard to get where I am," she said.

"So did I."

"You had a father to pave the way."

"A father you're convinced is a crook."

"Don't change the subject, Steele."

"I'm the youngest precinct captain in Manhattan. You don't have to tell me about ambition, Judith."

"Exactly," she retorted, "so don't jeopardize a job I fought so hard to get."

"And one you'll go pretty far to keep?"

"I don't know where your accusations are coming from this morning!" she managed, her voice tight, her body quivering against his—whether from anger or desire, he wasn't sure. "But if you think you can talk to me this way, you're wrong." Her eyes bored right into his. "Now, I want you to leave before my boss sees you."

"He won't. He's out to lunch."

"How do you know?"

"I checked. I know a guy at the front desk." Sully thought of Brave Dave and added, "We Steeles know a lot of people downtown."

"You checked to see if Joe was in?"

"Yeah."

Visibly, she relaxed. "Thank you."

Actually, he *had* been trying to protect her. "My job could be on the line, too."

Her voice was low, as if she half expected them to be overheard. "We could both get fired," she agreed. Her voice dropped another notch, but unfortunately, that only made it huskier and more enticing, and

Sully found himself leaning closer, as if to better hear it. As if he were a moth and she the flame...

"It's improbable," she continued throatily, while he tried to ignore how her voice seemed to enter his bloodstream. The sound enlivened every nerve ending, making his skin tingle. "But if someone wanted to push it to the wall for political reasons, they could call us in on the carpet for obstruction of justice, Steele."

"Sully," he corrected.

Ignoring him, she continued, "You seem to have forgotten I'm working on a case involving your father."

"I admit you're sexy, Judith," he began in a seeming non sequitur. His chest felt unbearably tight from drawing in the scent of her; bands of steel seemed to wrap repeatedly around his chest. "And yeah, I admit that right now, I'm thinking of last night...and the night before...and the night before that...."

"Stop this!"

He pressed on. "Most of the morning, while a heat wave was tripling the number of crimes in my precinct, I was thinking of you—how you looked last night, stark naked and wearing nothing but that robe for me."

He sucked in a quick breath as a vision of her filled his mind. He could almost see her breasts, perfect for the fit of his hands, the nipples dark and aroused. Hard and pebbly under the filmy transparent fabric, they'd constricted farther when he'd kissed them. Breathlessly, he'd taken in the nip of her waist, the flare of her hips and how her damp, sweet bush had looked, the dark hair curling and swirling into a perfect V. How she'd trailed her eyes over his naked body, staring at him with a hint of wicked lust.

She didn't look the least bit interested in him at the moment, however. In fact, she was starting to look as murderous as he felt. "And your point is?"

"That I admit you're sexy as hell, but I haven't forgotten you're out to convict my father. An innocent man," Sully added.

"One more reason you shouldn't have come here," she said pragmatically.

"No, that's exactly why I *did* come here." He eyed her a long moment, wishing he could fight the tantalizing heat washing in waves over his skin. He was hard, almost painfully aroused from nothing more than her near proximity, and from the memories of what he'd already shared with her...what he wanted to share again.

Guilt crossed her features, which didn't improve his mood. "You came down about the case? Do you have information?"

"Information?" His lips parted. "You don't give up, do you?"

She sent him a sideways glance. "Tell me what's going on."

"What?" he countered softly. "The way you told me you were delving into my bank account? Checking out my personal finances?" Trying not to register the warm feel of her breath on his cheek, he leaned back another inch. Not that it helped. She smelled of fresh wintergreen mints and looked dangerously kissable. "Did you really think no one would call me?"

She looked both stunned and innocent. "I'm looking into all the Steeles' records."

"All our—" He began explosively, then cut himself off. "Not just mine?"

She shook her head, and when the movement brought the reading glasses farther down on her nose, he had to fight the urge to pull them off. They marred her otherwise beautiful face, making her look too bookish. Too inaccessible. "I don't know why you're so angry," she said, gaping at him. "I got warrants for everyone."

"My brothers?"

"Everyone."

She stared at him another long moment, and he was sure she was gauging his reactions, wondering if he was hiding something. Feeling disgusted, he said, "That's you. A cop to the core."

"Usually," she reminded him, "it's what you like about me."

But not right now. The frustration was more than he could stand. "Nobody told me about the other warrants. Only about the one out on me."

"They were filed separately. Maybe the others haven't gone through yet. That, or your snitch only processed yours."

He cursed softly. No doubt he and his brothers would get calls about the others.

"No one should have told you anything!" she exclaimed. "As an I.A. official, I should question you about who squealed, but I know it's pointless. You'll never talk."

"You're right about that much," muttered Sully. "You're digging into our private records?" he added, still barely able to believe it.

"Of course. I'm looking at everything I can get my hands on. Your father was caught on tape taking seven million in public funds, and when I find him, it'll also be my job to take him down." She glared at Sully. *"Down,"* she repeated emphatically.

"We're not hiding anything." Sully's mouth set in a grim line. "I thought you'd started thinking he might be innocent."

"I don't think. I sift through evidence, just as you do. And just like you, Steele, I believe in concrete truths, such as the kind in hair samples and fingerprints. Look, just because we've been sleeping together—"

He told himself not to, but he grabbed her hand and threaded his fingers through hers. Once they were palm to palm, he could tell she was nervous. Muscles and sinews quivered, and despite their argument, Sully could think of a thousand other places he'd like to feel those long, slender, manicured fingers. "The fact that we're sleeping together doesn't matter to you?"

The pulse in her throat was ticking too fast, and he had to fight another sudden urge—this one to kiss that throbbing pulse point until she moaned. At his question, her eyes faltered, but after a heartbeat, they hardened again, looking like sharp, wet stones. "It matters. But not with regard to my case." Suddenly, she looked helpless, as frustrated as he. "You're a cop. You know how this works. Your father's in trouble. I'm the one who's after him. It's a case of the good guys versus the bad guys. It's that simple."

"Which am I?"

After a long moment, she shrugged. "I'm not sure yet."

"You're testing me, huh?"

"Isn't that what people do when they get to know each other?"

"No. Sometimes people just take pleasure in each other's company."

"Maybe some of us don't have that luxury."

He remembered what she'd said to him one day in his office when he'd challenged her. *Steele, you're wrong about me. I'm not made of ice.* "You'd take your own father down if you thought he'd broken one of your precious laws," Sully couldn't help muttering, reacting out of anger and instinct.

She looked momentarily startled. "What made you say that?"

"You didn't even bother to tell me you were getting the warrants."

Recovering from whatever shock she'd felt, she gave a soft grunt of frustration. "I'm not supposed to tell you anything at all. Joe would have my hide. You're lucky—*lucky*—" she repeated with emphasis, her voice rising, "that I've shared anything and—"

"I appreciate what you've done," he cut in.

Ignoring him, she continued, "I didn't have to call you when I was on Seduction Island, sifting through the remains of the *Destiny*. In fact, in case he didn't tell you, I threw your brother Rex off the island, threatening to arrest him for tampering with the evidence. I've made sure your brothers can't interfere. For you, however, I've made an exception. Please don't make me sorry I did."

She was right, he realized. He'd gone too far. For a second, he silently cursed the fact that he'd grown up in a family of rough-and-tumble cops. It didn't help that Sully spent his days in a precinct dominated by macho men whose lives were always on the line. Before he could say he was sorry for being so overbearing, she raced on. "I didn't have to tell you Tommy the Jaw owned the boat or Castle O'Lannaise, either. Hell, Steele, if I find your father and lock him behind bars, I don't have to tell—;

Despite his apologetic attitude, he'd had enough. Abruptly, his mouth slammed down on hers, and he stopped her with a hard, uncompromising, masterful kiss.

"Stop it," she grumbled, but not before he'd done what he'd considered doing moments before—taken off every last bit of her lipstick, leaving her lips red and swollen.

"For now," he agreed, his voice a tad milder, since the kiss had taken the edge off.

She exhaled a long, shaky breath. "Look, Sully, maybe it's better if we don't see each other for a while."

"Oh," he said dryly, thinking of the letters she'd written to him as Mr. X. "Now you're delivering the Dear Sully letter?" Last night, after they'd made love, he'd been about to tell her that he was the man corresponding with her, but he'd decided to wait. He'd wanted to do something romantic, maybe take her back to the bridge overlooking Bethesda Fountain, open a bottle of champagne and tell her as they sipped. Maybe, he'd thought, if things heated up and he decided to propose, he'd do so on the bridge and tell her then. But now...

"I just think," Judith began again, "with things as they are...I mean, given the fact that I'm involved with the case and..."

He could swear he saw fear in those marvelous blue, breathtaking eyes, but this time it wasn't because Judith feared he'd get her in trouble at her precious job. And it was precious, Sully realized. Whatever had happened to her during her growing-up years in Oklahoma had toughened Judith and made her hard. She was as tenacious as a pit bull. It was a good trait in a cop, but maybe not so good in a prospective wife. Catching the stray thought, he sucked in a quick breath. He kept his voice remarkably cool, given the fact that he was fighting panic he'd prefer not to acknowledge. Was she really going to end the relationship? "Not see each other?"

She nodded quickly. "Until the case is resolved."

"You're scared," he murmured, speaking his thoughts aloud, "but not because you think Joe'll find me here and you'll lose your job."

"Don't be ridiculous, Sully. That's exactly what I'm worried about. Harvard wasn't exactly inexpensive, you know. I'll be paying off my student loans until the end of time. I need this job." She sighed. "And I like it." After another pause, she added, "I *love* it."

"If it was money you were after," he said thoughtfully, "you would have gone into private practice, not taken up residence at Internal Affairs." He narrowed his eyes, knitted his eyebrows. "Why didn't you pursue something more lucrative?"

"Like I just said, I love my job. For whatever reason, it's in my blood. And don't probe. You're the one under investigation, not me."

"So you keep reminding me." Returning to their earlier topic, Sully brought his face closer, so he was peering through the lenses of the glasses, into her eyes. "You're afraid because I'm getting too close to you. You're afraid of me, Judith. As a man."

She didn't move, but the distance was there, anyway, in her eyes. All at once, she was looking at him as if he were a million miles away. "That's ridiculous, Sully," she murmured, but he knew he'd hit the nail on the head. "I'm just saying it's best if we don't see each other for a while."

"In your dreams."

Her eyes widened, just enough that he noticed how blue the irises were, almost as dark as the pupils. "You're refusing my request to take some time off?"

Time off. She was talking about their affair as if it were a job, but he tried not to react. "You sound like you want a little vacation," he said, his voice deceptively mild. It was tempting to push the metaphor and say something cutesy about her taking off for Hawaii or Florida, or some other resort area, but he somehow refrained.

"Yes, that might be best."

"I don't think so," he replied simply. "I'll see you at your place when you get off work."

Her sigh was abrupt, exasperated. "And if I don't let you in?"

"There are countless options," he murmured, determined not to let her get the best of him. "Lock picks. Or flashing my badge at the building's superintendent. Don't forget, I'm a cop, too."

"And I could arrest you for doing either of the things you just mentioned."

"You could," he shot back. "But you won't, Judith."

She looked annoyed enough to circle her desk, get a set of handcuffs from the desk drawer and arrest him right now. "What on earth makes you think I won't take legal action against you?"

"This," Sully said simply.

And then, angling his head, he closed his hard, hungry mouth over hers again.

7

How they wound up in bed again, Judith would never know. Actually, she did. Just as he'd threatened—or promised—Sully was waiting inside her apartment when she got home from work. As furious as she'd been at the intrusion, she'd shuddered when his arms circled her waist; her own had instinctively wreathed his neck.

The rest was history. Lovemaking had been rushed and urgent, spurred by the heat of their argument. Sully seemed afraid she really would break up with him, and all night, as if to convince her otherwise, he'd urged her to stay with him, using every sensual trick in the book.

Now, early the next morning, their clothes, not to mention most of the bedding, were still on the floor. She curled against him, her mussed hair spreading over a pillow and otherwise tickling his bare shoulder. Slowly, she stroked his chest hair—smoothing it, then catching it in fistfuls and mussing it, only to pet it flat again.

"You're going to make us late for work," he said.

She smiled. "We're already late."

"You're loving every minute of it," Sully remarked agreeably, grinning and shooting her a teasing glance.

"You have a bad attitude toward women, Steele."

"Not really."

She merely grunted. Then she sent her own eyes downward, inhaling sharply as she took in his nude body, her gaze following the movement of her hand as it glided over the pelt of hair bisecting his pectorals. With a nail, she traced the narrowing line of hair to where it arrowed around his navel, then brushed a hand where he was starting to get aroused again.

"Yesterday in your office, I was serious," she suddenly said in a whisper. She didn't want to give Sully up, not when she'd gone so long without a lover, and not when she felt half in love with him. But things were getting too complicated. "We should quit seeing each other."

Sully merely chuckled softly, increasing her pique, since he didn't seem to be taking her very seriously. "I can tell you're a woman of your word," he retorted. His eyes glinted with amusement as he grazed a hand all the way down her bare back, not stopping until he cupped her bottom.

"You were in the apartment when I got home," she argued. "You left me no choice."

His eyes sparkled, bright lights igniting in the amber depths, and he nodded sagely, his lips curling into another smile before he dipped his mouth to brush a kiss across the top of her head, further disheveling hair that desperately needed the business end of a comb. He grinned again, flashing white, even teeth. "Somehow, you figured out just what to do with your intruder, didn't you?"

Heat rose in her cheeks at the memories. "I tried to throw you out." But once he'd convinced her to let him stay, she'd suggested they take a bath together to cool off from the heat. "Anyway, I'm a cop," she admitted playfully, still stroking chest hairs that felt like freshly spun silk. Using the tip of her finger, she drew circles around his nipples, then fought a shiver as she watched them grow taut. "After law school, I went to the academy, and I graduated at the top of my class. They taught me a few things about how to handle intruders, Steele."

He released another chuckle, his brows waggling with humor. "Sorry, Judith, but I don't think a police academy taught you the moves I saw you make."

"Sure they did." Judith laughed and dipped her hand downward to touch him intimately. "You give a whole new meaning to the phrase *hardened criminal.*"

Sully laughed out loud, his shoulders shaking, the sound full and rich, coming from deep within his chest. "Careful," he warned. "Or you might solicit an assault."

"I'll keep that in mind." That said, she made absolutely no move to stop tracing mindless swirls on his belly. A rush of satisfaction claimed her as his arm tightened around her bare waist. When his hand settled at the inward dip there, his long fingers stretched onto her belly and his thumb rubbed an answering circle in a hollow near her hipbone. She sent him a mock glare.

He smiled back. "What?"

She shook her head. "I was just wondering how a man can be so maddening and so..."

He released another deep, throaty chuckle. "Wonderful?" he supplied. When she didn't respond, he kept searching for the right word. "Satisfying? Effective? Funny?"

She chuckled. "You're driving me crazy, Steele."

"Sully," he corrected.

"Sully," she repeated, smiling. Sweeping her lips across his, she edged up on her elbow so that she could look down into his eyes—lazy seductive slits as he returned her gaze. Warmth filled her, and for a second, time seemed to stop. She was aware only of his steady breathing, the slow rise and fall of his chest, and those penetrating eyes.

Yet another slow smile stretched his lips, and when she saw it, her heart did a flip-flop. He looked so content, and it was all her doing. He said, "Does this mean we're friends again?"

As she snuggled against him, merriment bubbled in her throat; she loved the easy banter they always shared. "We weren't *not* friends, Steele."

"You keep trying to break up," he protested.

And yet they kept winding up in bed. "I didn't know we were going steady."

He pulled her on top of him, opening his legs so hers fell between them. Circling his arms tightly around her bare back, he sighed as her breasts settled against his chest. She warmed her feet on his. "We're definitely doing something significant together, Counselor," he said huskily.

Scooting forward so she could rest her elbows on the pillow on either side of his head, she gazed down at him for a long moment. "I wasn't suggesting that we never see each other again, Steele," she said, her voice turning raspy, then hitching with need as she felt him growing aroused beneath her. "Just that we might want to back off...at least until I get some leads on your father."

There was a long, pregnant pause, then Sully said, "I've got something to tell you."

She squinted. "What?"

"He's alive."

The words came out of the blue. Her jaw dropped. She felt the air push from her lungs. "Alive? What are you talking about?"

"Just what I said. He's alive. I started to tell you before, but..."

Inhaling sharply, Judith struggled up so she was sitting on the mattress. Had Sully just said Augustus was alive? Her mind whirled, barely catching up. One minute she'd been cuddled in his arms, about to make love again. And now he was saying... "Alive?" She could only gape at him. On a rush of emotion—half excitement, half fury—she lifted the transparent curtain of the canopy, hopped out of bed and found her robe. Not that it did much good. The fabric was as opaque as Saran Wrap. Nevertheless, she pointedly tied the belt.

Sully had edged upward, so that he was leaning against the headboard. "Please," he said. "Get back in bed."

Putting her hands on her hips, she merely glared at him, determined not to let him sweet-talk her this time. Nor would she let herself be affected by the appreciative male gaze he was leveling at the robe. Yesterday, in her office, she'd weakened. He'd kept kissing her, and by the time he'd left, her knees were barely able to support her.

Later, when she'd found him in her apartment, not to mention in her bed, she'd tried not to give in. But she'd wanted him. Even now, just seconds after realizing he'd been lying to her, she wanted him. She hated herself for it. How could her own body betray her—craving a man who was going to cause her nothing but trouble?

"How long have you known?"

"Rex found out while he was on Seduction Island."

"Seduction Island!" Judith exploded, unable to contain her anger. As she continued talking, she began pacing, snatching up his clothes from the floor as she moved. Once she'd rolled them—navy jacket, trousers and briefs—into a ball, she tossed them through an opening in the curtain that surrounded the canopy. Change from his pockets rained down and settled in the thick pile of the carpet. "That's over a month ago! You've known your father was alive for more than a month? How could you have kept a secret like that?"

Pulling on his shirt, he began to button it. "Calm down."

"You lied to me."

"I omitted the truth," he admitted, stepping through the curtain and donning his slacks. Grimacing as he pushed his hands into his pockets, he glanced down at all the coins, but decided this was no time to pick them up. "I only wanted to buy time, so my brothers and I could—"

"Find him?" She stared at him. Beneath her surface

emotion was a whole other layer of hurt. Deeper and darker, it was pushing upward through her body. She had to get Sully out of the apartment before he saw the anguish she carried inside her from past betrayals. And yet she needed to hear the whole truth first. Tears pressed against her eyelids, not that she'd let them fall. "Did I really just sleep with you?" she muttered, unable to believe what a fool she'd been.

"Judith..." Completely dressed now, he slipped into his shoes as he came toward her. Stopping, he curled his hands around her upper arms. "Look at me."

Steady eyes met his. "Get out, Steele."

It didn't help that Sully looked uncharacteristically helpless. She was used to him being strong, competent and in control. "I'm not leaving until we talk. If I'd known you'd react by throwing me out, maybe I wouldn't have told you."

"You'd keep lying to me?"

He blew out a short sigh. "I don't know."

"You've known for over a month that your father is alive?" she repeated.

Sully's eyes pierced hers and his lips parted in unspoken frustration. "Can't you understand the torn loyalty I feel?"

"What a fool you all must have thought me," she mused, ignoring his question, "that night when I had dinner at your mother's." And to think she'd been fooled. Everybody there had known Augustus was alive, just as she'd suspected. "Where is he? And is there some reasonable explanation for why he hasn't come forward?"

Sully's broad shoulders lifted in a shrug. "All I know is that he's alive. That's all Rex found out on Seduction Island."

"I don't believe you, Steele."

"Don't be suspicious, Judith. It's the truth."

"How could I believe that now?"

"I know how you feel—"

"Why wait until now to tell me?"

"Because I wanted to talk to him before I.A. puts him in a cell. But I trust you and I want your help." Everything in his gaze said the time they'd shared in bed had something to do with the confession. For that instant, she was sure she'd moved Sullivan Steele's heart in some deep, permanent way. "After the *Destiny* exploded," he continued, "Rex stayed on Seduction Island. He was undercover, posing as a guy named Ned Nelson. Do you remember him?"

Oh, she remembered "Ned," all right. "Tall," she muttered, "with shaggy blond hair." He'd been prone to wearing tasteless, garishly printed shirts with khakis.

This explained how Rex and Pansy Hanley had spent enough time together to get engaged, Judith realized. On the island, she had frequently seen Pansy with "Ned." Apparently, the two men were one and the same.

Somehow, Judith managed to keep her cool. For a month she'd been on the island, feeling sure she'd forced Rex to back off from her investigation! "I should have guessed," she said. She worked for Internal Affairs, after all. More than anyone, she knew about Rex Steele's reputation as a master of disguises.

"Oh yes," she added, nodding her head rapidly. "I bet you all were very amused."

"At fooling you?" Sully grunted softly. "That's not the case, Judith. This isn't a game. We're trying to find Pop. We love him. Pulling the wool over your eyes doesn't figure into our motives."

But everyone at Sheila's had known Augustus was alive—except her. Judith wasn't proud of it, but more than ever, she wanted to solve the case. She hated being taken for a ride by police officers who had things to hide.

"Help us," he said.

"Have you told me everything?"

He nodded. "Yeah. Now I have. And if I get any word about where Pop is, I'll let you know."

"You really don't know?"

"No."

She took a deep breath. When their gazes met and held, she suddenly wondered what she was going to do next. She'd been about to throw Sully out—she knew she had to—but she couldn't stand the thought of never having him in her bed again. She stared at him, wavering. Her chest felt tight, constricted. Her throat was raw, aching with unshed tears. Why couldn't she find one man who wasn't a traitor? One cop who was really a good guy?

"Sully, I'm sorry, but I'm going to have to ask you to leave."

"Judith," he said simply. It was only a name, but his tone loaded it with emotion. She heard frustration, passion and a protest. She could swear she heard love, too, but that was probably only wishful thinking.

As she pointed toward the door, she tried to sidestep some of the coins, wincing as a penny stuck to her bare heel. "Please go." In case he didn't understand she was serious, she added, "Withholding the information that your father's alive really is obstruction of justice, Steele. If you don't leave my apartment, I'll slap you with a fine. Worse, if I can."

She hated the way he was looking at her. His eyes—the rich, golden color of autumn leaves—were too knowing. Just looking into them, she felt as if someone were reaching inside her chest and wrenching out her heart. He was sizing her up, gauging whether it was in his best interest to try to stay—and she could see the second he decided he'd really better go.

"This isn't over," he said quietly.

She watched him turn on his heel, then listened to his steps as he crossed the living room carpet. The sounds were followed by a barely audible click as he opened and shut the front door. As soon as he was gone, she swayed against one of the posts supporting the bed's canopy. Her heart was hammering, beating a fast, steady tattoo, and her eyes ached, but she wasn't going to cry. She couldn't cry. She hadn't cried over a man since she left Oklahoma, and she definitely wasn't going to start now, with a man like Sully Steele.

Taking a deep breath, she concentrated on mobilizing her emotions, determined to channel them into something positive and productive. "I've got to get to work," she muttered.

Work.

Yes. That was her usual solution. Deep down, she feared that if she gave in to heartbreak, by lying down and having a good cry, she'd never get back up again.

She was out of the shower and dressed in a black skirt and simple white blouse when the phone rang. Her heart lurched. *Probably Sully,* she thought. Maybe he was outside and calling from his cell phone to try to make things up. Would this really be the end of their affair? Had she seen him for the last time? Under the circumstances, she had to end it, and yet she wanted him back, too! Her heart was pulling in two directions and the experience was maddening.

As she snatched up the phone, she shuddered, remembering how warm and wonderful Sully's hands had felt when they explored every inch of her. She didn't bother to keep the pique from her voice. "Yes?"

"You're late this morning."

She started, her fingers curling more tightly around the phone receiver. It was Joe Gregory. He'd never called her at home before. She imagined him in his office, which was an exact replica of hers. An older, distinguished man, Joe was months from retirement, and like most cops who'd fast-tracked themselves into desk jobs at Police Plaza, he had sharp eyes that had seen too much of the world, and a receding hairline, since most of his gray strands had been claimed by worry. "Joe? What's wrong?"

"Nothing. But you're late," he said again.

It was bad enough that Sully had upset her, she thought, leaning to pick up the mess of coins on the floor as she talked. Having her boss act strangely was too much. Usually, she reached the office well before other staff members, and she left later, also.

"I believe this is the first time I've ever been late," she managed to say in her defense, although she refrained from stooping to compare herself to other, less punctual employees. "And I'm on my way." As she added the lie, she glanced down and suddenly squinted, her eyes landing on a small key that must have been mixed in with the coins in Sully's pocket.

Bending, she lifted and peered at it. Stamped with a logo from the Varrick Street post office, which was where she had her box, the key was identical to the one headquarters had helped issue for her, so that she could accept anonymous messages from troubled police officers.

Of course. As a precinct captain, Sully would have a similar mailbox. And if Augustus was trying to contact him, he might use it. It was a long shot, since Sully probably checked the box daily, but it was worth a try. She had to find Augustus. Until the case was solved, Sully would have to stay out of her life....

Unfortunately, the key was worn, and some of the numbers weren't visible. All Judith could make out was a seven, and what could have been an eight or a nine. She wasn't proud of it, but today might have to be one of the few occasions on which she'd use the combination of her good looks and badge to get information without a search warrant.

"Oh, I realize you're usually the first one here," her

boss was saying. He paused. "I don't really know how to bring this up, but I just got a call from a contact in the criminal records department who said he saw you and Sullivan Steele going into Jen Pang's restaurant in Chinatown the other night."

Fear rippled through her. Bracing herself, she wondered if she was about to get a reprimand. "Uh, yes, sir..." She searched her mind for excuses. "I can explain everything—"

"Totally unnecessary," Joe cut in. "I just wanted to commend you on going the extra mile with this case."

So that's why he'd called! Her lips parted in unspoken protest. Did her boss really think she was dating Sully in order to get information? Even she knew she had a reputation for being tough—but did people truly think she'd go that far? She bit back a frustrated sigh at the misunderstanding. "Thank you, sir," she murmured, "but if you'll just let me explain—"

"No buts, Judith. I knew you'd do a great job. Have your, uh, strategies been effective? Have you got any new leads from getting closer to Sullivan?"

Realizing defending herself was useless, she hesitated, once more silently cursing Sully for muddling her mind. She didn't know whether she was reacting because she was angry with him, or simply frustrated because she'd never been late for work, or because her boss had caught her in bed with the enemy.

"Some leads." Hedging, she considered telling Joe about the warrants that would allow her to look at the Steeles' bank accounts. But she'd wanted to wait until she broke the case and could surprise him. Hopefully, the warrants would all come through today. Judging from the fact that Sully knew about one of them, they were in the system, being processed. "I don't know, Joe." She gave another sigh. "I'm beginning to think Augustus really might be innocent. You know him. What's your take on his character? Anything beyond what you've already told me?"

Joe sighed in turn. "Not much. But..."

Sensing hesitation, she pounced. "What?"

"Judith, he's my ex-partner."

Used to cops who didn't want to talk, she chewed her lower lip. More than anyone, she knew that officers, even her boss, hated snitching on partners. Out in the field, these were men they had to trust with their lives. "That's what you said when I asked you before," she finally continued, "and I know you don't want to say anything to disparage Augustus, but we do have a video of him taking the money. What were you going to say?"

There was another long pause. "Just that back when we were working in Chinatown, there were some rumors about him being on the take. And during the trial, when Tommy the Jaw turned state's evidence for him, he..."

Her heartbeat quickened. "Yes, sir?"

"He...well, he implied to me that he'd taken some mob kickbacks."

Her heart sank, and as she acknowledged the feeling, she silently berated herself for getting emotionally involved with the case. Her job was to review hard evidence, not to decide guilt or innocence on the basis of emotion. "Thank you for telling me." She added, "I do have one piece of new information." She paused. "Augustus Steele is alive."

There was a longer, more pregnant pause. "Can you fill me in?"

"That's all I've got."

"When this is over, there'll be a commendation for you."

She almost hated how good the praise made her feel. Maybe Sully was right. Maybe her job meant too much to her. Shouldn't she be making more time for fun? For love? *For Sully?*

She pushed aside the thought. "I'm not after a commendation, sir," she insisted, wishing she, just like Sully, wasn't feeling so torn. She'd hate to see the look on his face if he knew she was passing this information along. And yet, she told herself, he would understand that this was her job. "The real satisfaction," she forced herself to add, "is in a job well done."

"Well put," agreed Joe. "You say you're on your way into the office?"

She glanced down at her outfit, then at the mailbox key in her hand. "Actually," she said, "I'm hoping you won't mind if I'm a few more minutes late. I...need to stop at the sixth precinct and track down Sully again. Maybe I can find out something more."

"In that case, take all the time you need."

"Thanks. See you shortly." Hanging up, she knew she wouldn't need but an hour, just long enough to get to the Varrick Street post office and check Sully's mailbox.

JOE GREGORY'S HAND remained tightly curled around the recradled phone receiver. Slowly, he withdrew it, leaning back in a roller chair identical to the one down the hallway in Judith's office. He stared out the window at Police Plaza, his eyes settling momentarily on a bride and groom heading toward the courthouse.

"Sullivan and Judith," he murmured, his mind on another couple. He should have guessed. He'd handpicked Judith for the job of tracking Augustus because, when it came to convicting cops, she was so ruthlessly ambitious. He should have known she'd cozy up to one of the Steele brothers....

"Smart girl." She was doing exactly what Joe wanted. Bringing down one of the Steeles wouldn't make her popular around New York precincts, of course, but then, Judith had always said she wasn't here to win popularity contests. Arresting cops won her respect, anyway.

She was feared, too.

Yes, Judith Hunt, quite simply, loved prosecuting men who were supposed to be heroes. And Joe was the only person who knew the real reason why. He figured it was good information to have, in case he ever needed to use it against her.

Now he just had to make sure he was around when she found Augustus. After all, if Augustus was doing what Joe suspected, Joe needed to make sure his ex-partner would never blow the whistle. Make sure *by any means necessary*.

The words played in his head. When he'd gotten home last night, Joe had eventually realized his house had been ransacked. Oh, it had taken an hour or so, since nothing had been moved or disturbed. Only someone as good as Augustus could have pulled off the break-in—getting silently past Joe's high-tech security system and two German shepherds.

And he'd found the book.

It was small, with an old red-leather binder. The contents were in code, but anyone who cracked it would find himself reading a detailed account of how dirty graft and protection money was moving through Manhattan nowadays. It would be the biggest police shake-up since Serpico.

No doubt, Augustus had taken the book. And wherever he was now, he was probably still in possession of the seven million dollars that Joe had spent a lifetime squirreling away. Joe wanted the book and money back where they belonged—in his possession.

Who would have guessed, all those years ago in Chinatown, that Joe's own partner—the man he most trusted to watch his back—would be the one to try to take him down?

Not that Joe was going without a fight.

8

SEVENTH AVENUE WAS renamed Varrick Street as it entered the neighborhood known as Tribeca, the location of Robert DeNiro's famous restaurant, and the place where David Letterman was rumored to live. Not that Judith was thinking of television and movie stars. She was thinking of Joe Gregory. With any luck, she'd have more information for her boss when she got to work.

Guilt assaulted her, and the more she felt it, the more she wondered if she wasn't falling in love with Sully. Even though it was her job, she didn't want to do anything that might wind up hurting him, including finding his father. And yet she had to....

Every time she thought of Sully, her heart fluttered and her insides turned as warm and runny as ice cream on these New York dog days. From the moment she'd left her apartment, she'd been fighting not to run down to the sixth precinct, fly into Sully's arms and make up with him. That was love, wasn't it?

But it's too soon to tell. You've only slept with him a few times, her mind protested.

It doesn't matter, came the answer in what was proving to be a never-ending internal argument. Regardless of the length of the affair, she and Sully couldn't keep their hands off each other, right? Whenever she thought of him, she craved his touch with astonishing hunger. Desire gnawed at her, compelled her, intrigued her. Besides, she and Sully had worked together for years, hadn't they? They knew each other from cases and police-related functions.

Not to mention that she'd always respected him as a cop. Deep down, she was sure what he said was true—he was as clean as a whistle. It was her job to be suspicious, but in reality, his precinct hadn't been issued any citations since she'd been with I.A. And Sully Steele cared about his men....

Just as Joe cares about me.

Judith had been lucky to wind up with such a good boss, and despite her feelings for Sully, she really hoped she could deliver the goods today. Dodging the crowd on the sidewalk, she kept her eye on the front door of the post office, which was nearly within reach now.

"I just hope it's air-conditioned," she muttered under her breath, slipping out of her suit jacket, slinging it over her arm and wishing she hadn't worn stockings. The August air was pushing at her in sweltering waves. Thick and muggy, it was pungent with street scents she'd just as soon ignore. It would be nice if one public building superintendent had ignored the mayor's edict and kept the temperature hovering below a hundred degrees. And if she could coax a clerk to compare keys and give her the mailbox number.

I'm here. "Thank you," she whispered, blowing out a sigh of relief as she sped through the door.

Bliss descended with a cool whoosh as she reached inside her handbag and pulled out Sully's key. Unfortunately, the air in here wasn't as icy as she'd been hoping, but it was significantly cooler as she headed toward a postal clerk.

Fortunately, he was male. And fortunately, he gave her an appreciative glance. Better yet, he was young, only in his twenties and probably not going to be inclined to ask to see a search warrant. His eyes widened when she flashed her badge and the mail key. "This is an emergency," she said in a hushed tone. "I'm from NYPD Internal Affairs and need to get in this box. Now."

She slid the key across the counter. "There's not much time. Some of the numbers have worn off, but some are readable. Can you match this up? Maybe give me the whole number?"

"Sure," he said easily. "Be right back. This is one of the older boxes. The keys are usually a darker gold. It should be easy."

She'd never imagined it would be this simple. "Thanks."

Speaking over his shoulder as he headed for the pegboards holding duplicate keys, he said, "Anything for the NYPD. My mother used to have drug dealers in her neighborhood in the East Village. You all stepped in and cleaned up the place. Used to be, she was too scared to go to the corner deli after dark."

While the clerk was gone, Judith glanced around and had an unwanted flash of memory. She was on one of the long drives her family used to take to the post office in Oklahoma. Because they lived on a farm, they'd always picked up mail, rather than had it delivered, and the post office was small, a one-room affair with only one clerk window and so few mailboxes that, when Judith was a little girl, she could count them all in under a minute. Pushing aside the vision, she turned her attention to the man as he approached.

"Thanks again," he said a moment later as he returned the key with a slip of paper. "I figure you probably need a warrant, but I won't tell if you don't. Like I said, I'm glad my mother can go out at night again."

"Glad to hear it," said Judith.

And then she glanced down, frowning at the slip of paper on which he'd written the box number. "Box 987? It can't be." That was Mr. X's box number.

"I'm sure that's right, ma'am. I double-checked."

She started to ask him to check once more, but curiosity drove her to look. It was a long shot, but maybe the man had received her last letter and canceled his box. She headed for her own, settling her eyes on the number: 11202. Glancing above and below, she gauged the direction she needed to go and quickly headed down the wall toward 987.

"Ten-o-seven...ten-o-six..." Her voice trailed off. "Nine sixty-eight...nine seventy-four..."

She stopped. "Here." Jiggling the key in the lock, she twisted it and opened the tiny door. Her heart missed a beat, and her teeth closed down on her lip. *Impossible.* Unable to believe her eyes, she tried to steady the hammering of her heart.

Only one letter lay inside.

It was the letter she'd written right before she'd gone to meet Mr. X. on the bridge overlooking Bethesda Fountain. As she snatched it from the box, betrayal knifed through her. Ever since the clerk gave her the number, she'd been hoping there was some mistake. Now her mind sped back to the day she'd spied the amber bottle near the bank of the Hudson.

Even now she could remember how she'd painstakingly made her way off the pier and through debris to get to the bottle. She'd been wearing high heels, and had nearly twisted her ankle. Still biting her lower lip, holding back a soft cry of anger, she imagined Sully standing nearby, surreptitiously watching her. He must have been pleased as punch.

So, he'd planned this. It was the most devious ploy she'd ever come across—and even worse, it had almost worked. He was a masterful cop, known for many things, including being an ace at interrogation. No doubt he'd guessed how lonely she was, how love-starved, and he'd thought that, if he wrote her, she would open up about her cases to a "pen pal."

The truth was, it had been tempting. She'd actually considered doing just that. Not that it mattered now. Covering all his bases, Sully hadn't stopped at letter writing. He'd slept with her, too.

Slamming the door, she crammed the letter in her shoulder bag and headed toward the exit.

She was going to the sixth precinct.

SULLY ROSE from behind his desk the minute he saw her. "Judith. Come in. Nobody told me you were on your way up."

She strode over the threshold, and in spite of how they'd left things this morning, Sully felt a rush of pleasure, figuring she'd come to the precinct to patch things up. The thought perished when he heard her tone.

"Told you I was coming up? Is that what you need when you see me, Steele? A warning?"

Not about to rise to the bait, he said, "Anybody ever tell you that you're a challenging woman?"

"Sure." She didn't look impressed. "Most people."

"Well, I'll add something else. I like it."

Unperturbed when she uttered something darkly unintelligible and hardly encouraging, Sully circled the desk and leaned against it, just as she had when he'd visited her office the day before. In spite of the tension coursing between them, he could still appreciate how the crisp, tailored white blouse she wore under her suit jacket hugged her body, and how the black skirt hit her thighs in just the right place—long enough to be tasteful, short enough to show off a pair of the prettiest legs in Manhattan. Of course, he preferred the white, see-through robe he'd last seen her wearing....

He cut to the chase. "You still sound pissed off at me, Counselor. I was hoping the intervening hour or two had put me back in your good graces."

"Watch your language."

"Sorry, I'm in cop mode," he replied, the apology genuine. "You surprised me."

"It was intentional."

He almost smiled. "As if I'd be up here in my own precinct, breaking the law."

"You never know."

Everyone in the sixth precinct knew he usually got

a call from downstairs when Judith Hunt visited. It was the standard drill. Usually, he would have had a chance to put on his suit jacket. Dark brown and serviceable, it was still slung around his desk chair. It was more rumpled than it should have been, and given how intently Judith was scrutinizing him, Sully wished he'd chosen a better suit; after their fight, he'd gone to his own apartment, showered and changed.

As if she'd read his mind, Judith said, "I told the guy downstairs that if he called you, the way he usually does, I'd slap him with a fine. I also told him I'd double it if he referred to me as Lips."

Sully pressed his tongue to his cheek. "So you know about your nickname, huh?"

"Sure."

Crossing his arms over his chest and wondering where this visit was leading, Sully raised an eyebrow. "I don't know if the law recognizes the offenses you named, so on what pretext were you going to write up the poor guy?"

She flashed a quick, insincere smile that made him wish for one more tender. Right about now, Sully would kill to have her look at him the way she had this morning before all hell had broken loose. She said, "I'm from I.A. I'd think of something."

"Ethical of you," Sully returned dryly.

"You're one to go around preaching ethics."

"I'm sorry about this morning." He sighed, dragging a hand through his short hair, which was slightly damp from the heat. "I should have told you Pop was alive. And..." He paused, thrusting his hands deep into the pockets of his brown trousers. "I know you could legally cite me for obstruction of justice, Judith. If that's what you choose to do, I'll understand. I'd never fault you for it. Withholding information was wrong. He's my father, but regardless of what you think, we Steeles have always lived by the book—"

She glanced over her shoulder, and he followed her gaze. Every man in the squad room had stopped working and was silently staring through the open door, the upper portion of which was glass. "Great," she muttered.

Sully's heart missed a beat as she stretched out a leg so long, shapely and mouthwatering that he wished they were in her apartment again, cuddled in bed. Catching the toe of a high heel on the door, she kicked it shut—so hard that Sully winced, half expecting the glass to shatter.

When it didn't, she flicked her wrist, drawing his attention to the flash of a silver bracelet and the long sexy fingernails that, not so long ago, had been busy exploring choice parts of his anatomy. Too bad the clouds in her thunderous blue eyes said she'd just as soon shoot him as look at him. She could, too, he supposed, given the fact that she carried a gun in her handbag.

She flicked her wrist once more, and this time she grasped the cord to a venetian blind. The last thing Sully saw before the blind rattled, dropping all the way down to cover the glass portion of his door, was the surprised expression of his sergeant, Nat McFee. Nat was right outside the door, at his own desk, and just moments before Judith arrived, he'd asked to see

Sully, saying he'd tracked down something important about her.

That had happened only seconds before Judith had stormed into the squad room. Now she was stalking toward Sully, her high heels tapping on the tile floor and her slender hips rolling in an incredibly womanly way that belied the angry pursing of her crimson lips.

"Go ahead," he said again. "Cite me for obstruction."

"You're not going to be that lucky, Steele."

"You have worse in mind?" For a heartbeat, he thought she'd been toying with him, and that she really had come to the precinct to suggest a truce. Maybe she was about to settle that creamy, crimson mouth on his....

She came close enough that he was drawing in heady scents—something musky from one of the expensive soaps she kept handy on the lip of her bathtub; something fruity from shampoo that he'd used himself; something floral from a black-and-gold spritzer bottle she kept near the sink.

"Anyway, if I did cite you for obstruction, it wouldn't matter," she continued, sounding none too happy about that fact. "Your family has more friends around town than I could ever battle. Once the charges were filed, some committee or judge would shoot me down."

He could see now that Judith really was having a bad day. "Now, now," he countered in a chiding tone. "You know better than that. The system works. You arrest guys every day. If a Steele was really guilty, he'd go down hard, just like anybody else."

She shook her head as if no lawyer could convince her, including herself. "No, you Steeles always find some way to break any rules that don't suit you."

He had the strangest feeling that whatever was fueling her anger wasn't entirely about him. "We're cops," he tossed back easily. "We uphold the law."

She was starting to look as if she wanted to tear him apart with her teeth, but when she suddenly swung at him, Sully was taken completely by surprise. She was beautiful and feminine, and now that he'd been inside her apartment, Sully knew she pampered herself. It was unthinkable that she'd hit a man, even though Sully was aware she'd been trained to shoot one.

Lifting a hand, he easily caught her fist as it landed in his palm, sounding like a baseball hitting a mitt. Inhaling sharply, he took another second to fully register the impact of flesh meeting flesh. Had she really just tried to hit him?

"Judith," he murmured, his fingers closing gently over hers. He hazarded a quick glance toward the door before he simply reached out with his free hand and hauled her into his embrace. Being held tightly against his chest seemed to further upset her, though, and she punched him again—once, twice, raining blows on his shoulders that didn't really hurt him as much as let him know how much she wanted to.

"What's going on?" he whispered in confusion. Squinting down, he brushed heartfelt kisses into her hair, and then he glanced at the door again, hoping Nat made sure none of the men came in. Probably they wouldn't, but Sully would hate to have any rumors get started.

He was a man, so he'd get grins and claps on the back for making a conquest, especially since most Manhattan cops had probably fantasized about Judith. They respected her position, sure, but that didn't change the fact that she was stunning. She would suffer politically if she got caught in his arms, though. It was a double standard, and Sully hated it, but he knew it was the way of the world.

"C'mon," he whispered, cupping her shoulders and urging her to take a step back, just in case someone came in. "Talk to me. What's going on here? This isn't about this morning, is it?"

The gaze she leveled at him tore his heart. Her face looked so damnably calm. Too calm. Color had drained from her already pale skin, taking it a shade lighter, if that was possible. Those perfectly shaped, brilliantly painted red lips set off her sculpted ivory cheekbones, as did the midnight slashes of her eyebrows, not to mention those shocking blue eyes.

It was her eyes that really got to him. The irises had turned as dark as her pupils, the way they always did when she was mad, which was too much of the time as far as Sully was concerned. Instead of flashing angry fire, her eyes suddenly looked so soulfully wounded he could barely stand it. She looked like a puppy or a kitten or...

Dammit, he was a cop and shouldn't be reacting to this kind of look! Bracing himself, he gently squeezed her shoulders. He had no idea what was bothering her, what had happened or what she was going through, but if he could wipe that expression from Judith's eyes, he'd happily take on the pain himself.

He peered at her. "Do you want to sit down? Maybe go out for a cup of coffee? Did you eat breakfast?" Realizing he was rambling, he fell silent. He was asking every question under the sun, just hoping he'd hit on one she'd answer.

"Excellent interrogation technique, Steele," she said coolly, as if reading his mind.

"Yeah," he admitted. "I'm just throwing things out, hoping something will stick."

Her eyes sharpened. The wounded look vanished, and suddenly, those eyes were cutting into him. "I thought you really liked me, Steele," she accused, trying to hide the tremor in her voice.

He could swear tears glimmered in her eyes, too, but that was impossible. Women like Judith Hunt didn't cry. But what if she did? She had a reputation for being as tough as nails and as smooth as glass, and if she really did start crying, Sully had no idea what he'd do.

He took a deep breath. "I do like you, Judith." If the truth be told, his feelings were a lot stronger than that.

She actually seemed to retract, and his heart ached, because he could feel her distancing herself from him. Her tone was only slightly caustic, but he suddenly felt that everything was over between them, and pain sliced through him, so sharply that he barely registered when she said, "Oh, really?"

Feeling helpless, he lifted a hand and traced the smooth line of her cheekbone with his thumb. "Yeah."

Was this the time to tell her? he wondered as he gazed down into a face he daydreamed about most of the time. Searching his mind, he had trouble finding words, but he wanted to remind her that they had so much to share. There were many points of connection—their temperaments, interests and work, not to mention the energy between them in bed. Their relationship could easily become so much more, maybe even everything....

Suddenly, he thought of the lottery money, and his mind ran wild. Had Judith found out about the deal with his mother? Had she decided he was trying to marry her to get his share of the fifteen-million-dollar windfall? Had she run into Trudy Busey? Or called Pansy Hanley to question her further about the explosion aboard the *Destiny*?

Either woman could have informed Judith that Sheila was making her sons wealthy, once they found brides. Was it possible that Judith had discovered everything hinged on Sully now, since Truman and Rex were engaged?

"You must think you're really slick, Steele."

"No," he said gently, hoping he wasn't about to lose her. "I don't. If you'll just explain...."

"Here." Stepping back, she pressed a letter to his chest. As his fingers closed over an envelope he'd recognize anywhere, his heart swelled with relief. So that's all it was. She'd discovered he'd been writing her love letters. Surely this could be cleared up.

"The mailbox key," he said. It had been in his pocket with his change. "I was going to tell you, Judith."

"Just like you told me your father was alive?"

"Better late than never."

She merely stared at him, challenging him with her eyes. When they fluttered shut for a second, he had another moment's heartbreak. Would he ever kiss those eyelids again? Feel the soft brush of her eyelashes against his lips?

She said, "Well, aren't you going to read it?"

Her gaze was boring into him as he opened it, and when he read the first words, he felt another small rush of encouragement.

Dear Mr. X,

Just moments from now, I'll be meeting you at Bethesda Fountain, and I hope I'll be able to find the right words to express what I most want to. Writing to you has meant so much to me. It's helped me open my life to new people. I want to learn to love so much more deeply and intimately.

And while that's true, and while you've meant so much to me, I don't believe you're the man for me. Since we began corresponding—

Hearing the door open, Sully lifted his gaze. "Judith—" He was just in time to see her walk across the threshold, shutting the door behind her.

He wanted to follow, but his hungry eyes fell to the paper again:

—I met a man I believe I could fall in love with. As it turns out, I've known him for years. We work together and I deeply respect him. We just seem to click, and last night, we slept together for the first time. By then it was too late to cancel our meeting. Just in case these words don't come together in the right way when we meet, I really want you to know how important you've been to me—

Dropping the letter to the desk, Sully headed for the door. On a morning when he'd been busy putting out fires all over his precinct, maybe this was just one more. Surely Judith would accept that her finding the message in a bottle wasn't only a strange coincidence, but one more reason they should be together. Fate had dictated it, and Sully had been waiting for a romantic way to tell her. With a rush of hope, he registered that she'd been meeting Mr. X. only as a courtesy. She wanted to be with *him*—Sully.

When he opened the door, he was relieved to see she was still here. At least until she stared up from whatever she was reading on Nat McFee's desk. Her lips were pulled so taut that she could have decided never to utter another word again in this lifetime. And even worse, as Sully started toward her, she turned on her heel and ran.

Squinting, he reached the desk, needing to know what had happened before he chased her. When he saw the open file, he felt his heart miss a beat. There were two clips, one from a weekly Oklahoma newspaper, the other an office newsletter from a precinct where her stepfather, Officer Jonathan Haviland, had worked. Apparently, Judith had kept her deceased father's surname.

Feeling sick, Sully scanned the pages, realizing that

Judith hadn't enrolled in high school her senior year because the summer before she'd accused her stepfather of rape. The man was a local cop, but luckily, a local female lawyer, Suzanne Beckett, had believed Judith's story and pushed for a trial.

It was over quickly, though. Too quickly for justice to have been served, Sully realized. To get a conviction would have taken more time. Rape, after all, was the hardest crime to prove. And one of the most damaging to the victim.

Especially if the perpetrator is a father figure in a caretaking capacity. Sully set his lips grimly. He'd bet the stepfather's cop buddies had turned a blind eye to any evidence they'd found. Judith was right. Some cops really were dirty.

"No wonder she works for I.A.," he whispered. Given what Judith had told his mother during dinner, he figured Judith had never talked to her own mother or stepfather again.

A victim of rape.

On the job, he'd seen it far too often. He knew better than to give in to blind rage, however. That would be all too easy, but it was never of any help to the victim.

The victim.

Judith.

My lover.

Sully didn't even want to think of how often he'd loved her without knowing. Why hadn't he asked her to explain the occasional lapses in attention during their lovemaking? Or what he'd sometimes taken to be her lack of experience? Or how she'd sometimes braced herself against him, as if she were afraid? Each time, there'd been a reasonable explanation....

But there was no excuse for him not asking. His eyes felt gritty. "Oh, hell," he muttered softly.

"You found the file?" Nat said from behind him. "Sorry, Sully. I feel lousy. You and I both know that's the last thing we expected to find."

"Shred it," Sully said simply, sweeping the file from the desk. "Make sure the other guys don't see it. This is Judith's personal business. If she'd wanted it known, she'd have made it public. And now I want her protected."

"Right, Boss."

Sully barely heard. He'd already gone after Judith.

9

"JUDITH."

His voice was low, but it carried in the cavernous garage. Speeding her steps, Judith edged between two parked cars, then around a large white support column, toward an open door. Up ahead, strong beams of sunlight were streaming inside, and she could hear horns blaring and engines revving. Hopefully, there'd be plenty of available cabs. She just wished she'd gone to Police Plaza and signed out a city car before coming to the precinct; she could have simply gotten into it and driven away. Now, Sully might catch her before she could get a cab.

"Judith," he said again.

He was closer now, almost right behind her. Knowing she had no choice, she turned around, her hand instinctively pressing against a column behind her. She steadied herself against it, glad they weren't in sight of the glassed-in attendant's booth. At the moment, the last thing she needed was an audience.

When her eyes locked onto Sully's, he stilled his steps. He was six feet away, but as far as she was concerned, it wasn't anywhere near far enough. Definitely, it was the wrong time to notice how good he looked. In his button-down shirt, with its rolled-up sleeves and loosened tie, he appeared harried, important and competent—just the kind of man she needed as a friend.

And lover. Memories of last night crowded into her consciousness, and her heart felt as if it were swelling inside her chest. She'd never felt so close to anyone. Naked in an embrace, skin-to-skin, their bodies had been hot and damp, their arms and legs twined around each other. He'd been buried deep inside her, and while he'd barely moved against her when they made love, every inch of her had shuddered. For the first time in years, she'd felt she belonged to someone again. She was his.

"Don't come near me, Steele."

"I won't do anything you don't want me to do."

She should have known he'd say something like that. He'd had years of experience dealing with victims. Tears pushed against her eyelids, making her eyes sting and her throat burn. Determined not to let them fall, she took a deep breath and managed to say, "How comforting. Guess you learned that response in a textbook."

He merely nodded. "Among other places."

"I'm not somebody you're meeting during a domestic disturbance."

"No. But you could have been."

It was the truth, and she hated that he'd read those articles. He was so in control, too, so nonplused when she tried to push him away. Her belly clenched, and she realized she was shaking inside. She was starting to panic, wondering what was true, what was false. Was Sully her greatest protector? Her truest lover?

Was he the man fate had sent to bring love into her life?

Or was he just another traitor wearing a badge?

Probably. He'd researched her background to get information he could use against her if she prosecuted his father. He'd left a message in a bottle where she could find it, so that she'd tell him about her case. Worst of all, he'd seduced her, making her trust just enough that she almost believed he really cared.

Feeling her throat tighten, she knew she had to get out of the garage soon, away from Sully Steele and his comforting presence...away from those strong arms that could wrap around her and protect her. Away from a body that seemed designed to come between her and harm. She had to get away from those caring amber eyes. Warm and watchful, they were scrutinizing her with concern. Looking into them, she was sure he'd do anything in the world for her.

And she was just as sure that was a lie.

"I'm so sorry, Judith."

Sorry? How could such a simple word contain so much meaning? Pain twisted inside her as her mind raced back in time. Her father had been long dead when a new daddy—one sworn to protect and serve—had swept into her life wearing a badge and a uniform. He'd transformed her and her mother's lives. He'd taken them to parties, bought them dresses and a new car, and helped with farm chores—slopping hogs, weeding gardens, gathering eggs from the chicken house.

And then when she was seventeen...

A sob almost tore from her throat. The event itself

had been over in a heartbeat, but she could still smell the alcohol on his breath. How could mere moments affect so many years of a woman's life? And why hadn't anyone helped her? Her mother? The police? Someone?

"I'm sorry," Sully said again, and Judith snapped back to the present, realizing he was holding his hands palms-out at his sides, as if he'd be glad to pull her into a hug at any second. Yes, his arms were right there, waiting, and she could run into them if she wanted. She could almost feel them—how the muscles would flex as his taut forearms curled around her back. His hands would splay on either side of her spine as he drew her close.

He cleared his throat. "Judith...when we make love..."

Heat flooded her cheeks. Was there something wrong with her? Had he guessed all along how scared she'd felt? Should she tell Sully that even though she'd been scared sometimes, what he'd done for her was magical and wonderful? "It's over between us. Why talk about it, Steele?"

"Because I don't want it to be over," he said, his voice husky with emotion. "I want to be with you in whatever you're feeling right now, Judith. I want to build a sensual life together, and to make that better for you. The best."

Silently, she damned him for knowing just what to say. Just what a woman who'd felt so betrayed and injured might want to hear. Emotional hunger filled her when she thought about having dinner at his mother's house; the Steeles pulled together and supported each other, and that night, they'd seemed like the loving family she'd craved for so long.

"Stop it," she said in a near whisper. She had to do her job. Fifteen million dollars was still sitting in Sheila Steele's bank account. Since all the Steeles had known Augustus was alive, each was guilty of withholding information that could lead to the arrest of a felon.

"Can you talk about it?"

Hadn't she wanted to? she wondered, her mind pulling back to the subject. Secretly, hadn't she wanted Sully to know about what had happened to her?

He'd taken another step forward. He must have inched nearer when she hadn't been watching. "Damn you for treating me like we're in a hostage situation, Steele." Yes, he was definitely moving toward her steadily, just as they'd been taught at the academy. She could almost hear the drill instructor. *Move slowly, using your feet, not your upper body. Get close before they realize you're there. Keep eye contact with the victim.*

"Aren't you?" he asked gently, the softness of his voice edging out the past, reminding her of the new memories he'd given her...of sweet seduction and sweeter pleasure. "Aren't you a hostage to your past?"

"Just drop it, Steele. Let me go," she said, but she knew he was right. Ever since she fled Oklahoma, she'd been ruled by the past. She'd fought back, going to law school, then the academy. Unlike Judith's mother, Suzanne Beckett hadn't turned her back and accused Judith of lying, and watching Suzanne do what she could to battle the good-old-boy network had made Judith determined to follow in her footsteps. She might be able to help others....

When her case was dismissed for lack of evidence, Suzanne had brought Judith into her home, helping her finish high school in a neighboring town while she applied for scholarships. Now, anytime Judith convicted a cop, she knew that deep down, she was also convicting another man....

When Sully took yet another step forward, she tried to back up, but with the column behind her, there was nowhere to go. She bit back a sound of frustration. Why couldn't Sully react the way so many men would? Why couldn't he make a rough joke? Or minimize what she'd been through? Maybe pretend that an event such as she'd suffered wouldn't haunt her?

Even indifference would be easier to deal with. No, she didn't want to get any closer to this man. She couldn't! "You researched my background." She'd expected her voice to shake, and when it didn't, she was glad. Her voice sounded strong, angry and righteous. She needed that show of self-respect, that control. "You were looking for bargaining chips, in case you wanted to use something against me, weren't you, Steele?"

"I was trying to protect my father."

Now he looked as if he wanted to protect *her*.

Lies, something inside her screamed. *Don't look into those kind, probing eyes. Don't fall for it. Don't believe he's trying to help you.*

Her voice was still astonishingly steady. "While

you were busy researching me, you seduced me, Steele. You made your way into my bed—" *Into my heart.* The thought came unbidden, and she rushed on. "Because of your father. You did everything you could to protect his interests."

Every time Judith gauged his distance, Sully was closer. It seemed as if he were floating toward her, magically advancing without even moving his feet.

"There's some truth in what you're saying," he admitted calmly. "At first, protecting my father was a part of my motive. But as I said before, things changed."

"Stay right there!" she suddenly demanded, her free hand gripping her shoulder bag as if touching its smooth, gold clasp could steady her. She needed to hold on to something—anything! Anger was bubbling up, getting the best of her. "You got Nat to research—"

"I did." Sully cut her off, but his tone remained reasonable, almost unbearably so. "I've asked him to shred the documents, too. None of the other men saw them. I understand how delicate this is. How personal."

The gesture touched her heart, but she pushed away the sensation. "What do you want, Steele?" she ground out. "A medal? If you hadn't been digging into my background for purposes of blackmail, then you wouldn't be in a position to make such a protective gesture. Right?"

"I understand your point."

"Damn you," she swore again under her breath. Every time she challenged him, he kept his cool. It was hard to keep hating him when he looked so collected and kept his tone so deceptively mild.

Don't let him fool you. Don't let him in, not on an emotional level. She'd seen the file on his assistant's desk. She'd caught Sully red-handed.

In a flash, she recalled the accusations in her mother's eyes all those years ago. She felt everything slide off-kilter, and suddenly, Judith really didn't know what to believe. How could you believe your own version of the truth when the people who supposedly loved you denied it?

"Were you standing on the banks of the Hudson?" She pushed on forcibly, as if mere words could help her hang on to her own reality. "Watching me when I made my way down to the riverbank? Did you get a big kick out of watching me fumble around in the mud to get that bottle out of the water?" Her eyes pierced him. "You planted that bottle there, didn't you, Steele?"

With a start, she realized he was right in front of her. "Can I touch you?" he asked simply, quietly.

She ached at the words. Yes, she wanted to be touched by the big strong hands that hovered right above her shoulders. She wanted to feel them cup her arms while his thumbs rubbed the hollows near her arm sockets. When she didn't respond, he did just that, grasping her so lightly that she could have been made of glass. The gentle pressure of his fingers imparted a world of care.

All the breath seemed to have left her body. "You planted that bottle there for me to find."

Peering deeply into her eyes, he slowly shook his

head. "No. I really didn't. I was thinking about marriage, about wanting a wife when I wrote the letter, put it in a bottle, took it to the pier and threw it in. Fate brought it back to shore, Judith. And fate made you find it."

She could almost hear his voice speaking the words that played in her head. *Dear Lady of my Dreams, why haven't I met you yet? If only I knew where to find you, sweet lady, which city blocks to wander, which cafés to visit...*

As if reading her mind, Sully softly said, "Maybe I passed you a thousand times without recognizing you." Stroking his fingers along her smooth cheek, he cupped her face. "If only I knew what your face looks like...a face I'll hold between my palms and see resting on a pillow if you really turn out to be the lady of my dreams."

"I'm not the lady of your dreams, Steele," she managed to declare as his hands dropped away. "You dug into my past. You seduced me. You went out of your way to strike up a correspondence, thinking I'd inadvertently give you information about your father."

"That's not true. And I'm not *him,* not a man who's done you wrong," Sully replied simply. "I'm not another man in uniform who can't be trusted. I'm on your side, Judith. Never forget it."

She felt pulled in two directions. Was he a true lover or a seductive traitor? "I'm leaving, Sully."

As she turned away, she heard him say, "Before you go, you need to know one thing."

She shot a last glance over her shoulder. "What's that?"

"I love you."

Her heart wrenched. She desperately wanted to believe those words, but the man who'd married her mother had said them, too. So Judith murmured, "Goodbye, Sully Steele."

And then she walked away.

"THANKS," Judith murmured as the cab pulled to the curb in front of Police Plaza. Blindly, she dug into her purse, past her gun, and found her wallet, then pressed some bills into the money tray built into the Plexiglas partition between the seats. "Here. Keep the change."

The cabbie grunted his thanks. "Need a receipt?"

"No." Usually, she'd wait for one, since the city would reimburse the cost, but she was already opening the door, determined to keep moving. Before she broke down and cried—*if* she broke down and cried—she wanted to be seated comfortably in her office, surrounded by familiar things: leather-bound law books, the polished cherry desk she sat behind every day, and the view she'd gotten used to seeing through the window. After the scene with Sully, she needed to be in her own domain.

No matter how hard she tried, her mind couldn't piece things together. Should she trust him or not? Did he really love her or not? *Forget about him, Hunt.*

Her steps quickened as she approached her building, and she suddenly wished she had sunglasses to hide the redness of her eyes. Not that she'd wind up crying. She never did. She'd been through too much over the years, and she'd learned a long time ago that she could endure just about anything.

Work helped.

Relief filled her as she pushed through a revolving door, flashed her badge at a security desk and walked toward the elevator. Soon she'd be at her own desk, surrounded by familiar files and knotty problems that needed to be solved.

Thankfully, the elevator doors opened immediately after she pressed the button, and better yet, the cab was empty. It was cool, too. Outside, the day was proving to be another scorcher, and the fresh white blouse she'd donned not two hours ago already felt damp with perspiration.

Just don't cry, she schooled herself. *Keep busy.* She should be grateful she had a lead: Augustus Steele was alive. She needed to focus all her energy on that this morning.

By the time the doors opened onto her floor, she'd decided to go straight to Joe Gregory's office. Since he'd called her at home, she should tell him she was here. From what he'd said, she should question him further about his partnering days with Augustus, too, something that might help get her mind off Sully—and what he'd learned about her past. Had Sully really said he wanted to give her a better sensual life?

Her heart lurched. She wanted that, not that she wasn't already satisfied. She'd like to believe Sully was in love with her, too. Still, as a lawyer, she'd been trained never to trust what people said, much less a man like Sully Steele. After all, in the world of words, truth could be twisted into countless shapes, like a child's balloon at a county fair.

Unlike words, evidence never lied. Hairs, fibers and fingerprints were even better than polygraphs. All Judith could hope for was to find hard evidence in the Steele case. Suddenly, she tilted her head. She narrowed her eyes when she heard her boss's voice rising in anger.

"No...yeah, I want it." There was a pause. "Meet...tonight...cut a deal..." After a longer pause, he added, "After dark. Ten o'clock..."

Was Joe plea-bargaining a case? Meeting a snitch? Stopping in her tracks, Judith glanced around. She hadn't run into any co-workers yet. The halls were empty, as were the offices she'd passed. That wasn't unusual—it only meant people were in court—but she slowed her steps instinctively, lessening the sharp clicks of her heels.

She stopped outside Joe's closed door. His voice was coming from the crack beneath it; she couldn't make out any words now, but her boss sounded edgy and scared. His pitch rose and fell unnaturally, as if he feared being overheard.

"...Battery...City...Rector..."

Slowly, she strung together the words. Joe was planning to meet someone at Rector Park, a patch of greenery that opened off the riverfront walkway at Battery Park City, at ten tonight. But why? Joe was senior enough that he usually left fieldwork to younger people. This didn't sit right. Not that Judith didn't trust her boss, but...

He hung up the phone. Shaking her head to clear it,

she quietly backed toward her office. She'd nearly reached it when her phone began ringing. Great. What if Joe opened his door and heard her pick up? Would he guess she'd been eavesdropping? And was her gut instinct right? Was Joe involved in something underhanded?

"No," she whispered. Surely it was nothing, and yet the call had sounded so surreptitious. Leaning over her desk, she lifted the phone receiver. "Hello?"

"It's Sully."

His voice alone made her melt, but she knew she had to be tough. "I can't talk, Sully. I'm on a case that involves your father."

"This time it's not about us—"

It cost her, but she managed to say, "Save it, Steele."

"No, I need to talk to you about the case. You need to know—"

She simply couldn't stand listening to his sexy, husky voice, one she'd heard while he nibbled on her ear, whispering countless sweet nothings. Leaning forward once more, she quickly hung up the phone.

10

NINE FIFTY-FIVE.

Five minutes until show time. From a crouched position behind a bush, Sully glanced up from his watch to survey Rector Park. Rectangular in shape and landscaped in a classical style, the park had two identical, arching wrought-iron entrance gates positioned at its east and west sides. Inside the squat, well-maintained hedge that surrounded the park, four identical banks of shrubbery decoratively bracketed the park's corners.

Sully was stationed behind the bushes in the southeast corner. Truman was stationed at the northeast corner with his fiancée, Trudy, who'd insisted on coming along, determined to break a story for the *New York News*. Rex was waiting diagonally across the park from Sully, hunkered down behind the bushes in the northwest corner, closest to a walkway that ran along the Hudson River. Pansy, Rex's fiancée, had returned to her Realty job on Seduction Island, but Rex had stayed in Manhattan, saying he couldn't quit the force until Augustus was cleared.

Hopefully, that would happen soon.

Funny, Sully mused. All the brothers' love lives were riding on whatever happened next. With any luck, in just a few minutes, Trudy and Truman could put their wedding plans into motion, Rex could feel free to leave for Seduction Island, and maybe Sully would get another chance with Judith. Pain seared through him when he thought about what she'd suffered, and how alone she must have felt.

Blowing out a long sigh, he shook his head and thought about his mother. Optimistic woman that she was, Sheila Steele was the only one who'd stayed home tonight. Convinced the tide would turn in the Steeles' favor, she was cooking a buffet of their favorite delicacies—ham-and-cheese hoagies, hot Asian chicken wings, New York style cheesecake, and margaritas. Earlier in the day, she'd tearfully—and joyfully—reunited with Augustus, and as everyone had filed out the front door of the brownstone to come to Rector Park, Sheila had sternly said she expected them home in two hours for their midnight snack.

Too bad Judith wouldn't be at the party. Not that there'd *be* a party unless everything went right over the next few minutes, Sully thought. All day, Rex and Truman had been giving him a hard time about Judith. The way his brothers saw it, they'd found fiancées, and unless Sully did also, none would be beneficiaries of the fifteen-million-dollar lottery win. Sheila had said all three of her sons had to marry or the deal was off.

"So, it looks like the money's going to the sea turtles," Sully whispered to himself, wondering if his mother really would send her windfall to the Galapagos Islands wildlife reserve as she'd threatened. He had a horrible feeling that things between him and Judith weren't going to work out.

Exhaling another surreptitious breath, he pushed the thoughts from his mind and did his best to stretch his legs without standing as he took in the park's six benches. Complete with black iron scrollwork, they were arranged so that strollers could enjoy two matching, rectangular flower gardens. Late summer blooms of red, white and blue created the perfect simulation of American flags.

Unaware of the Steeles' presence, Joe Gregory had been seated on one of the benches for the past twenty minutes, pretending to read the *New York News*. The only person in the park, Joe was wearing a gray suit he'd probably worn to work that day, and occasionally, when he glanced over the newspaper's top edge and scanned the surrounding streets for Augustus, Sully got a good look at his face, which was square with a chiseled jaw. Bits and pieces of him glinted under the light of a full moon—his teeth, a white button-down shirt, a few strands of gray hair.

Sully tried not to dwell on the old days, back when he and his brothers were kids and Joe their pop's partner. Joe would always wrestle with the Steele boys, or bring them candy, or slip them a buck. Who would have known he'd turn out to be a rotten cop? Yeah, Joe was one cool customer; Sully had to give him that. It came from years of police work. Early in the game, New York cops learned to put their emotions on hold, or else they never survived the mean streets.

Just like Judith.

Her mean streets hadn't been in New York City, of course, but the backwoods of Oklahoma. This morning, in the precinct's garage, Sully had seen tears gleaming in her heart-stopping blue eyes, making them appear unusually shiny and bright. He suspected she rarely—if ever—let such tears fall. For a second, he'd believed she was going to break down and ask him to hold her in his arms. He'd been sure her heart was thawing and her insides were melting. He could almost feel how much she wanted his love.

And how afraid she was to let him in.

Stop it, Sully. He couldn't afford to torture himself over her, especially not when some major action was about to go down. Still, he knew that the betrayal his family felt regarding Joe was nothing compared to what Judith had endured.

"Dirty cops," Sully whispered in disgust. Tonight, he hated them every bit as much Judith did. Judith, the woman he *loved.* As the word played in his mind, he acknowledged the truth of it.

At least the Steeles had each other to rely on. Blood ties, commitment, family. Years ago, Judith had had no one. Sully wished he could prove his father innocent, bring her into the family fold and let her experience how it felt to be cherished and protected....

Safety in numbers, he thought, glancing toward his brothers again. And then he bit back an unprintable oath and whispered, "Judith."

He should have known she'd show. She was too good at her job not to find out about this meeting on her own.... But from whom? And how much did she know?

Maybe not much. Groaning inwardly, he watched as she paused under the wrought-iron archway on the opposite side of the park. Squinting into the darkness, he could barely make her out. Her black clothes blended into the hot summer night, as did her dark hair, which was pulled tightly back from her face. Before tonight, he'd only seen her wear suits, a dress or nothing at all—never baggy jogging pants, a T-shirt and sneakers.

Edging forward, he ventured farther from the cover of the bush while still staying in the shadows, hoping to signal her. From where she stood, a shrub blocked her view of Joe. No doubt she thought the park was empty. Rex was closest to her, but not close enough to warn Judith away without blowing his cover....

Sully could only shake his head. He'd tried to reach her all day to inform her of this meeting. Shortly after she'd left the garage, his mother had called, asking him to come home. When he'd arrived, he'd found his brothers there—along with Augustus and the missing seven million dollars. Augustus had told his version of the story, saying he'd wanted to involve the family as little as possible, so no one else would be implicated in the theft.

Pop had tried to meet Rex on Seduction Island, but hadn't realized he was disguised as a tourist, and hadn't even recognized his own son. Unable to find him, Augustus had finally returned to Manhattan....

Sully had hoped sharing that information would mend the rift between him and Judith. She'd refused his calls, though, and when he'd tried to track her down at Police Plaza, she'd eluded him.

How had she found out Joe was coming here tonight? Sully wondered again. Had her boss told her?

Maybe convinced her that she'd be helping him arrest Augustus? But why?

Whatever Joe Gregory was up to, it was no good. *Go back, Judith,* Sully thought. *Get out of sight before Joe figures out you're here.*

But it was futile. Sensing a presence and probably thinking it was Augustus, Joe suddenly turned. Seeing Judith, he rose, and oblivious of the true situation, Judith kept moving toward her boss.

"Joe?" Sully heard her voice rise over the breeze. "Is that you? Uh, what a surprise...."

So, Joe hadn't told her he'd be here. As the old cop turned more fully to face her, Sully could see him angrily crumpling the newspaper in his fists. Dangerous—maybe even murderous—displeasure crossed his features, not that Judith could see. The emotion vanished abruptly, replaced by a charming smile.

"Hello, Judith," he said amiably. "This is a surprise. What brings you here?"

Given the engaging tone, they could have been chitchatting at a police politicking dinner. Judith was striding toward her boss, and with every step, Sully hoped she'd hang back, that she wouldn't get within arm's reach. Joe Gregory, head of Internal Affairs, was not only a dirty cop, but also a deadly one. As it turned out, he'd nearly killed Augustus Steele....

Still seemingly oblivious, Judith said something Sully couldn't quite make out, then added, "I was out jogging...."

Joe's voice carried more easily. "You don't live in this area, do you?"

"No, I don't," she said quickly, "but I like to jog in

Battery Park City because the riverfront's well policed. And when I saw you here..."

She was stalling. Somehow, she'd found out about this meeting on her own, and now she was checking things out for herself.

Despite the circumstances, Sully realized *he* was checking *her* out. His eyes drifted over her tall, lithe, shapely body. Aching, he suddenly felt sure he'd never feel her next to him again—warm, aroused and in his arms. He wanted to love her and help her heal. Swallowing hard, he eyed her fanny pack. If there wasn't a gun in the bag, maybe she was wearing an ankle holster. He hoped so. If everything Augustus said about Joe Gregory was true, Judith might need a weapon.

"Well...thanks for jogging over to say hello," Joe was saying. "I do live in the neighborhood, and I often like to take a walk at night. Do a little reading..."

As if anyone would come to a dark, empty park to read a newspaper, Sully thought. Worse, Judith was the department's top prosecutor, so Joe knew she'd never fall for such a ridiculous ruse. Nevertheless, the man had been under extreme pressure ever since Augustus had called this morning, telling Joe he had the red book and the money in his possession, and asking for this meeting.

Right now, Joe was likely to say—or do—anything. Which was why Sully was relieved to see Judith take a step backward. Realizing he'd been holding his breath, he slowly exhaled. "Thank you," he whispered to nobody in particular.

Maybe she intended to get to higher ground, to observe whatever was going to happen next. Sully just wished there was some way he could alert her to his presence, but he couldn't risk being seen.

She'd almost moved beyond Joe's reach when Sully heard the click of footsteps on the dark sidewalk just outside the park.

Augustus had arrived.

"AUGUSTUS STEELE," Judith whispered, feeling sure the chips were falling into place. "Of course."

In the moonlight, she could easily identify the man she'd often seen around Police Plaza. He'd paused under the wrought-iron archway nearest South End Avenue, opposite the archway through which she'd entered the park. He was wearing jeans and a simple white T-shirt that accentuated his stocky, muscular, tough-guy frame, and with his high forehead, hooked nose and narrowed eyes, it was nearly impossible to imagine him fathering three tall, lean, handsome sons. No doubt Judith wasn't the first to decide the Steele boys had gotten their good looks from their mother.

At least Sully, Rex and Truman weren't here, Judith acknowledged with relief. That meant they probably weren't involved in their father's criminal activities. Determined not to let thoughts of Sully break her concentration, she dropped her gaze and took in Augustus's beefy hands, which were fisted around the handles of two suitcases—the same cases he'd used when he took the seven million dollars from People's National Bank. She recognized them from the incriminating videotape.

Her breath caught. Was the missing seven million dollars inside? Had it been in Sheila Steele's account? If so, was the remainder of the fifteen million still there, too? Or had Augustus brought that to the park?

"Why isn't he coming closer?" she whispered.

Joe said, "I told him I'd meet him alone."

She winced, hearing the barely suppressed censure in her boss's tone and realizing she might be blowing a major bust. "Sorry."

Joe's voice was tight. "You should be."

She could have kicked herself. This morning, why hadn't she simply asked Joe about the conversation she'd overheard? "You were talking to Augustus on the phone this morning. I should have known," she murmured.

It made perfect sense. Running from the law wasn't easy, especially not when Internal Affairs was involved, so Augustus had decided to surrender. As both his ex-partner and head of I.A., Joe was the perfect contact to bring him in.

Usually, Judith would have been champing at the bit, asking Joe if he'd made a plea bargain, exchanging lesser charges for Augustus's confession. Instead, her heart swelled, and where it felt larger and emptier, quickly filled with hurt. Sully was going to be crushed....

His father was a criminal. And she sympathized, Judith thought, pushing away memories of the moment she'd realized who—and what—her stepfather really was.

Why couldn't Sully be spared betrayal? Was there any way she could lessen his grief? She wondered if there would be anything she could do...and if their affair was really about to end. She was sure that prosecuting his father would be the last straw.

"I wish you'd told me," she forced herself to say to Joe. "I was assigned to the case. I probably should have guessed, though. You know Augustus better than anyone." Regardless of the identity of the perpetrator, she supposed she felt a rush of renewed respect for her boss. It was hard to arrest ex-partners. Her eyes still on Augustus, who hadn't yet moved from his position at the gate, she said, "When I heard you on the phone today..."

"You knew I was talking to Augustus Steele?"

"No, I didn't know it was him, and I was worried because—" Cutting herself off, she decided this wasn't the best time to tell Joe she'd been afraid he was in trouble. It had sounded almost as if someone was blackmailing him.

"Stick close to me," Joe said as Augustus took a step through the archway.

Obediently, she inched nearer. "It was decent of you to agree to meet him here alone, Joe." Coming without backup was risky, but this way, Augustus could be brought to justice with the least amount of police and press, which would be good for both him and the NYPD. It had taken some public relations know-how, but so far, the press had kept a low profile; higher-ups in the NYPD hated to look like fools. Before the story broke more widely, they'd wanted the missing money found.

Beside her, Joe was murmuring, "Yes...exactly right, Judith. You're so smart. This is so hard for all of us. I mean, Augustus and I have such a long history...."

So, her boss had been steps ahead of her all along, as had often been the case during her stay at Internal Affairs. Joe, after all, was very seasoned and generous about showing the ropes to newer employees. "I understand why you didn't ask for backup," she said cautiously, not wanting to offend a senior official. "But Augustus may be dangerous."

"Exactly," replied Joe quietly.

Yes, Augustus had come to the park, possibly carrying seven million dollars in cash. Unless something else was in those cases. Maybe he'd even brought all the money he'd stashed in his wife's bank account. Her years of involvement with the police had taught Judith one thing: criminals rarely acted logically. She shook her head, wishing her warrants had come through, since that paperwork might have helped Joe....

Once more, she felt glad Sully wasn't here to see his father handcuffed and hauled into a jail cell. Augustus was now coming toward her and Joe. When he spoke, his voice carried easily on the steamy summer night, sounding unbearably like Sully's. Low and so oddly calm as to be called gentle, it emanated from deep within Augustus's barrel-like chest. Squinting into the darkness, Judith could almost imagine that Sully—not his father—was out there, calling out to her from the bushes.

"You said you were coming alone," Augustus challenged.

"Ms. Hunt said she was jogging and saw me," Joe answered.

Augustus was now near enough that Judith could hear him utter a disgruntled harumph. "Likely story." As he stopped before them, he added, "I kept my end of the bargain, Gregory. I came by myself."

"Mr. Steele," Judith stated calmly. "We've seen each other before around Police Plaza. I'm from Internal Affairs. What Mr. Gregory says is true. He didn't know I'd show up...."

"I'll wager he didn't," Augustus said with a soft chuckle and a dry tone, neither of which made sense, given that he was about to turn himself in. Very slowly, bending only his knees, Augustus lowered himself and set down the two suitcases, so gingerly that they could have held bombs instead of a fortune.

Joe spoke to Augustus. "Since you're worried about Ms. Hunt's presence, maybe she'd better go."

A sharklike smile curled Augustus's lips. "You mean before I hand you the red book you're so interested in?"

Judith frowned, glancing between the two men. "What red book?"

"Gregory...!" That was Sully's voice. Whirling toward it, Judith found herself staring at a clump of bushes in the park's southeast corner. As low and deep as his father's, Sully's voice seemed to burst through the thickly pungent heat and the night's inky darkness. "Gregory," he shouted, "we've got you covered."

Covered?

That made it sound as if they were about to arrest

Joe. Why was Sully here? What was he talking about? Judith's heart hammered as she looked from her boss to Augustus, then to where Sully was stepping from his hiding place. He was wearing dark clothes, so while his frame was large and muscular, he was nearly lost in the shadows. He was nothing more than a silhouette under a flash of silver moon, but still Judith's heart ached.

She whirled again when another Steele shouted, "You're surrounded, Gregory."

This time it was Rex. Nearer to Sully, Truman also stepped from behind a wall of shrubbery. "You won't get away with this," he vowed.

The Steeles sounded so sure of themselves, so righteous! Definitely, they were accusing Joe of something. Narrowing her eyes, she scrutinized her boss, concentrating on his expression. "What's going on?" she demanded.

"Quite a lot," said Augustus grimly.

"Don't listen." Joe's face was placid, his tone smooth and calm, possessing the same command for which he was known at work. "These men are slippery as snakes. All the Steeles are in on this, Judith."

"All for one," Sully shouted. "And one for all. You're right, Gregory. Every Steele brother is here to take you down."

Ignoring him, Joe continued in a well-modulated voice calculated to inspire confidence. "The Steeles withheld information about Augustus being alive. You know that, Judith. And I saw the paperwork on your desk for the warrants. You were right to start checking into their bank accounts. I bet you found a pretty penny in there...."

For an instant, she'd been sure there was more here than met the eye. Surely, even if Augustus had stolen the money, Sully wouldn't be involved, would he? Doubt filled her as Joe continued, "Oh, you wouldn't believe how Augustus angled for me to hire him at Police Plaza years ago. Isn't that right, Augustus? It was only a matter of time until he asked—as helpfully as you please—to endorse and deposit checks for the Citizens Action Committee." Joe snorted with derision. "It was a routine part of his job, and years passed before I began to suspect the truth—that he only wanted the responsibility so he could skim money off the top."

"Graft money, Gregory," Sully interjected, his words even in pitch and carrying over the expanse of the park.

"Exactly," Joe answered reasonably, almost seductively. "Not everybody who pays into the Citizens Action Committee fund is honest, Judith," he explained. "Mobsters, grifters and burglars pay for police protection by making out checks to the committee. For years, Augustus has distributed the money to dirty cops. He makes the payoffs, then siphons his sizable cut into offshore accounts."

"*Your* accounts," Augustus corrected softly. Turning to Judith, he added, "Everything your boss says is true. But he's the criminal, not me."

Judith's mind was reeling, unable to quite catch up. Who was lying—the Steeles or Joe? "But you endorse and deposit the checks?"

"True," Augustus replied. "After that, it's Joe who controls the account, though." Pausing, he reached into his back pocket and pulled out a small book with a cracked red leather cover. "I know your reputation, Ms. Hunt. In fact, I've heard enough about you from my son, Sully, that I hope you won't mind me calling you Judith?"

Before she could respond, Augustus moved as if to hand her the book. "This is the proof you'll need to convict your boss. He's as dirty as week-old laundry."

"The Steeles want you to believe that, Judith." Joe's voice hitched nervously. "Keep listening. I bet they'll tell you it's a code book that, when cracked, will identify all the dirty cops around the city."

"And you know what, Judith?"

Once more, Sully's voice rode to her through the hot night air. She could barely see him through the inky darkness, but when she stared in his direction, she could swear their gazes meshed. She shook her head. "What?"

"He'd be right," Sully continued. "But Pop stole that book from Joe's house."

"Now, that sounds legal," Joe put in ironically.

She raised her voice, wanting answers. "What about the explosion aboard the *Destiny?*" she demanded.

"Pop already had circumstantial evidence against Joe. He was getting ready to contact you when he realized Joe was about to empty the committee's account and skip town."

Raising her voice, she directed the comment toward the bushes. "And your father beat him to the punch?" It was what the Steeles had wanted her to believe all along.

She felt, rather than saw, Sully nod. "You got it."

"And the *Destiny*?"

"You were right," Sully called. "Pop borrowed Tommy the Jaw's boat, meaning to hide the money at Castle O'Lannaise, Tommy's place on Seduction Island. Pop also figured he could meet Rex there. But Joe followed Pop and sneaked aboard. He tossed a little poison into Pop's drink, planning to grab the money and swim ashore after setting a timing device. The *Destiny* was supposed to explode—with Pop on it."

Sully paused. "Joe figured people would assume Pop was guilty and that the money had been blown to smithereens. Any remaining bills would have washed out to sea, right? Meantime, Joe was going to swim ashore with the cash. He'd go back to his office, wait until retirement—and then live the rest of his life as a very, very rich man."

"But I was tougher than you thought," Augustus added. "Right, *partner?*" He emphasized the word as if it was a curse. "Drugged as I was, I wrestled the money away, knocked you out and got off the boat. You were lucky you woke up before the bomb went off. I've hidden the money ever since."

"Lies," Joe said with disgust. "There's fifteen million dollars in Sheila Steele's bank account and you know it, Judith."

She was beginning to understand why the devil was said to have a forked tongue. There were so many plausible stories here, so many possible scenarios and interpretations. It didn't help that Augustus looked surprised.

"Fifteen million dollars?" he gasped. "In my wife's account?" Lowering his tone, he sounded venomous. "If you put money into my wife's account, hoping to frame me, or her, I swear I'll kill you, Joe."

"There *is* fifteen million dollars in your wife's account, Mr. Steele," Judith declared, just as her boss smiled, seemingly realizing he was in the catbird seat.

"It's money you stole from the Citizens Action Committee," Joe nearly purred. "Admit it."

"Sorry, Pop," Sully called out. "But we were sworn to secrecy. There is fifteen million in the bank. Believe it or not, Ma won the lotto." He added, "She really did, Judith." Just as earlier, in the garage, Sully was slowly moving closer. He was only twenty feet away now, edging around a flower bed. She watched as he stretched out his arms, as if asking her to run into his embrace.

"The lotto?" She swallowed around a sudden lump in her throat as she eyed Sully's very tempting open arms. "You expect me to believe that?"

"Oh, it gets worse," Sully replied easily, and even though it was still too dark to really see him, Judith could feel the slow, ironic twist of those lips that had kissed her senseless.

"Worse?" she prompted.

"Unless each of her sons marry within three months, Ma's donating the money to the Galapagos Islands wildlife preserve."

Judith was so shocked, she barely heard Augustus

harumph and mutter, "That sure sounds like my Sheila."

Judith could only shake her head. She'd seen Sully countless ways—raising Cain in his precinct, pursuing criminals and naked in bed. But she'd never thought she'd see him in a public park, asking her to believe such utterly insane lies.

Especially not when Joe Gregory remained the voice of reason. "Good try, boys. We appreciate your attempts to protect your father, but we've already caught him on videotape. He's guilty. With a full confession and the return of the money, we may be able to plead down his jail time."

"Nifty," murmured Augustus thoughtfully. "I go to prison for a crime I didn't commit, and you get off the hook—a lot poorer, but scot-free. Is that right, Joe?"

"A fifteen-million-dollar lottery win hasn't been publicly claimed." Sully was talking directly to Judith again. "It's been in the *New York News*."

She'd read the story. In fact, everything Sully said sounded plausible, if far-fetched. Or was that wishful thinking? Didn't she want Augustus to be innocent? And for the Steele brothers to restore her faith in the system? *To be a part of their family, too?* added another voice, from deeper within her.

Joe was scoffing. "Nobody *won* fifteen million dollars."

"But we Steeles *stole* that much?" Sully retorted. "Get a grip, Joe. We can prove that red book came from your house. We can crack the code, too. So you don't have a prayer."

"What if I did do it?" growled Joe.

Out of the corner of her eye, Judith saw his hand slip surreptitiously to his side. He was under too much pressure. He was going for his gun! One more heartbeat passed during which she hesitated. Who was lying—Joe or the Steeles?

She wasn't positive.

But she knew what she *wanted* to believe.

And for the first time in years, faith was enough for her. She had to start believing...caring...trusting again. She was already poised, her weight on the balls of her feet, and she took off at a sprint—toward Sully.

But it was too late! She was in midstep when Joe slammed a swift fist into her back, the punch cutting off her wind. As she gasped, his arm wrapped around her waist, squeezing out the remaining air. Her lungs burned. Her throat felt raw. She felt as if someone had stabbed her in the chest. He was older, but he was experienced and well trained as a street fighter, and with a flick of his wrist, he unclipped her fanny pack, slinging it toward a flower bed.

Now her gun was gone! Not that she had time to applaud herself on the correctness of her gut instincts. As the bag landed in the flower garden, she was busy wrenching, twisting her body, desperately squirming from Joe's grasp.

"Let go!" Why weren't the Steeles helping? Did this mean they were guilty?

Sharply, she elbowed Joe's ribs while grinding her heel into his foot. When he merely grunted, she lifted her chin to look around. "Do something!"

And then she whispered, "Oh." No wonder the

Steeles hadn't aided her. Joe was waving his gun—aiming at one brother, then another. When the pistol's bore swung toward Sully, Judith felt the horrific sensation of having her heart drop to her feet.

Sully was standing in the open! He could die! Regardless of who'd committed the theft, she realized she could never lose him. Her mind raced. They'd all been trained at the academy, and they all knew the same tricks, but she was known to play it by the book. Protocol demanded that, in a situation such as this, she not fight back. She was supposed to act nonthreatening by going limp in Joe's arms.

She pretended to do exactly that. Predictably, his grasp relaxed, and when it did, she wrenched again, harder this time. At the same instant, Augustus swooped down, grabbed one of the heavy suitcases and threw it toward Joe's face.

She ran.

"Sully!" She was barely aware she'd shouted his name, or that tears she usually never let fall were streaming down her face. He was only twenty feet away...then fifteen...then ten. But she felt she'd never hold him again.

Before she could reach him, his voice turned sharp, cutting through the night air like a knife. "Down, Judith! Get down! Down!"

A gun went off!

And then everything was jumbled. For a second, she thought she'd taken a bullet, then realized the impact was the bulk of Sully's body. He'd dived, hitting her broadside. "What—?" she gasped incredulously as the wind left her lungs for the second time in only a few short minutes. Sully had tackled her and lifted her clear off her feet; together, they were flying through the air. His shoulder took the shock as they went down, hitting the ground, and all she felt as they began to roll was the protective curve of his arms around her. All she could see was the hard, protective wall of his chest.

And then flowers.

No wonder it was so soft! They were rolling on a flower bed, over soft red and white flowers that smelled like heaven. When they came to rest, with him hovering over her like a guardian angel, nothing else seemed to matter.

Vaguely, from the periphery of her vision, Judith was aware that the other Steele brothers had closed in on Joe. As her boss had fired his weapon, Augustus had lifted the second suitcase, using it as a shield. In the melee, the case had opened, spilling its contents. Recording equipment had been inside, not money—which meant Joe had been taped. He hadn't confessed, but what he'd said was incriminating enough to be helpful. If the red book really did expose dirty cops, and if it could be linked to Joe, there'd be a conviction.

Somewhere, seemingly far off, Judith heard a woman's voice hitch excitedly. "Mr. Gregory, this is Trudy Busey from *New York News.* Would you like to make your statement at this time, sir?"

Whatever response Joe made, Judith didn't hear it. Sully was still on top of her, his big, warm body sending waves of heat through every inch of her. Just lying there together was obviously enough to start arousing him, too. With his legs settled between hers, she could feel him getting hard with desire. Still trying to catch her breath, and not caring that her tears were falling freely, she managed to quip, "I've heard of a man having a body like steel...."

"Sorry," he replied gruffly, threading his fingers possessively into her hair. He hadn't even cracked a smile at her play on words. Concerned eyes roved over her as he started to roll away. "I didn't mean to crush you, Judith. I wouldn't have tackled you, but I saw Gregory fire his gun and—"

"You wanted to protect me?" she finished, thinking, as she flung her arms around him, that he'd most definitely earned his nickname.

"Yeah. I did. I never knew what I'd do if you cried," he murmured, "but now I do." He began kissing away her tears, then simply gazed down at her. "You're so strong."

"Damn you," she whispered, crying harder as she wrapped her arms more tightly around his neck, so he couldn't go anywhere. "You're not crushing me. Don't you know I like feeling you on top of me, Steele?"

Surprised only for a brief second, he smiled. "Sully," he corrected hoarsely, bringing his lips so close that they lightly brushed hers. "You promised you'd call me Sully."

She smiled through her tears, the smile slow and wicked and curling the corners of her mouth just as his swept hers again. "Well, then, damn you, *Sully,*" Judith corrected.

His only response was a husky chuckle. And then he pressed his lips more firmly to hers, deepening their kiss in a way that promised a world of loving to come.

Epilogue

"YOU LOOK GOOD ENOUGH to eat," Sully murmured, looping a finger around the neck of a champagne bottle and carrying two glasses as he trailed his eyes over Judith. Made of plush crimson velvet, the simple, form-fitting dress she'd chosen for Pansy and Rex's Christmas wedding exactly matched her lips, as well as the bouquet of dark red roses in her hand, which Pansy had just thrown over her shoulder and which Judith had just caught.

Sucking in a breath, Sully settled his eyes where a sharp V-neck showed off the creamy paleness of Judith's skin to perfection and accentuated the rich, dark color of the hair curling on her shoulders. Hair, Sully thought, that he'd much prefer to see cascading over a pillow in their bedroom. Unfortunately, he'd only managed to get Judith halfway up the steps. So far.

"Good enough to eat?" she repeated with a soft chuckle. "Is that an offer, Sully?"

He tried to look scandalized. "What a dirty mind, Ms. Hunt."

She merely laughed, thinking of how the months of their sensual relationship was deepening the bond between them. "I credit you with that, Captain Steele."

"Credit where credit is due."

His grin was huge. Leaning over, he threaded his fingers through hers and pulled her another step upward, anxious to get her into their recently redecorated bedroom at Castle O'Lannaise. It was sumptuous, redone just as it had been in the days when the resort had been owned by Jacques O'Lannaise, a French pirate whom Pansy Hanley—now Pansy Steele—claimed still haunted the estate.

With plush, royal-blue carpeting and a round bed strewn with pillows, the room Judith and Sully were sharing had definitely inspired more than one good love scene since their arrival. French doors opened onto a balcony overlooking the ocean, and they also had a view of much of Seduction Island, including grounds of the magnificent adobe estate that Pansy and Rex would reopen in the spring as a public resort. Stables were visible, as well as an old, mysterious-looking watchtower.

Judith sighed at her good fortune in being here. "You're so wicked that I definitely should have you arrested," she murmured to Sully. Before he could respond, she playfully batted him away and added, "Now, don't be a pest. Let me read." With a last glance over the banister at the wedding reception taking place below, she resumed scanning a framed *New York News* article that was proudly hanging on the wall, midway up the steps. "Written by Trudy Busey," ran the byline, accompanied by Trudy's picture.

"'...Mrs. Steele was the recent lucky winner of fifteen million dollars in the city lottery jackpot. Wife of NYPD officer Augustus Steele, Mrs. Steele admitted she didn't publicly claim the money because she wanted to see if her sons—three more of New York's finest—could fulfill their part of her bargain: if each found a bride within three months, she would split her fortune among them. Otherwise, the funds would be donated to the Galapagos Islands wildlife preserve...'"

"'Of course, there were stipulations,'" Sully said, picking up where Judith left off. "'The three brothers, who've become known about town as the Big Apple Bachelors, couldn't tell their prospective brides about the deal. Also, they had to be in love.'"

Judith gasped. "You had to be in love?"

Trying to look surprised, she sent Sully a teasing smile, her eyes drifting over him, her heart squeezing tightly when she saw how good he looked. Because he'd been Rex's best man, he was wearing a simple black tuxedo, exactly the sort Judith wanted him to wear for their own wedding. "Does this mean you really love me?" she challenged.

"Sure," he replied easily, his eyes turning smoky with emotion. "But I know you don't completely trust that yet. Would you like to hear it again?"

"If you don't mind."

"I love you, Judith."

"I love you, too, Sully."

And she did. More than she'd ever imagined loving anyone. Maybe even enough that she could heal from the past. Sometimes a woman simply had to move on—opening herself to new people, making a family of her own. And the Steeles, Judith knew, were about to become that new family for her....

A few days after they'd taken Joe Gregory in for questioning, Sully had coaxed her to the bridge overlooking Bethesda Fountain. Once there, he'd knelt in front of her and proposed, withdrawing a ring box from his pocket and opening it, so she could view the diamond she'd been wearing on her left ring finger ever since. As soon as she'd said yes, he'd retrieved a stashed bottle of champagne and they'd toasted their future.

Now she frowned, her blue eyes glinting with amusement. "Your mother said you had to marry within three months, though."

"I think the timeline was close enough for Ma. Didn't I tell you she's decided to bend the rules and split the money among us, anyway?"

"Just checking," Judith teased. "You know I'm really a gold digger."

Looking thoroughly amused, Sully merely rolled eyes that glittered with merriment. "Oh, yeah, it really seemed that way this morning."

This morning, Judith had awakened Sully with the slowest, most sensual tongue bath imaginable. More soft laughter escaped her lips. "You have a point there, Steele." She thoughtfully added, "But it's too bad for all those sea turtles on the Galapagos Islands. There was an oil spill near there last summer, and I'm sure they could use help...."

"Good thing you brought that up," he said, trying to tug her upstairs again. "Truman and Trudy already decided to donate part of their share in Ma's name, and while Pansy and Rex need theirs to fix up this place, I was thinking that maybe you and me..."

Judith couldn't have been more delighted. "Could donate some to the turtles?"

He nodded. "Yeah. In Ma's name."

"Fine by me." Actually, money was the last thing on her mind; she had Sully Steele, and every day, she was more convinced that's all she'd ever need. Her eyes traveled to the framed article again.

"'...Mrs. Steele's possession of fifteen million dollars did, however, complicate many New York criminal cases,'" she continued, lapsing into silence as she read the news of Joe Gregory's arrest and conviction. The red book had been linked to Joe, and once cracked, the code had implicated a number of other New York cops. It had been a shame. But sometimes people decided to take the easy way out, without caring who they hurt in the process.

Day by day, as she got to know Sully better, Judith was becoming increasingly convinced that there was more good in the world than bad, however.

They'd all been relieved when Augustus hadn't even gotten a slap on the wrist, of course. Inarguably, he'd withdrawn funds that weren't his, and had illegally broken into Joe Gregory's home. But when all the facts were in, it was equally apparent that, had he not committed those crimes, money belonging to the state would have vanished. Since all Joe's ducks had been in a row—including bank transfers and travel plans—Augustus had been hailed as a hero. Now he was ready to retire in a blaze of glory.

Oblivious of her thoughts, Sully was shaking his head. "I bet Trudy was glad to finally break the story. She and Truman solved the Glass Slipper Case," he said, referring to a well-known case in the city, "and while she was working on that, she discovered Ma won the lotto. Everybody at *New York News* wanted the winner to be identified, but Trudy decided to keep mum until we all found brides."

Judith's eyes met his and held. "I guess it's okay to talk now." Pansy and Rex were married, and Trudy and Truman would be in the spring, as soon as Sheila Steele's garden was in full bloom again. And she and Sully...

"I can think of lots of things to do besides talk," Sully said.

She surveyed him, eyes sparkling. "I've noticed."

A very slow, very sexy smile curved the corners of his lips as he dragged her up another step and away from the framed article. They took one more step. And another. He said, "Thank heavens, Hunt. Now I'm getting somewhere."

"It's just too bad about Joe," she murmured as they reached the top of the stairs."

"It's a wedding day!" Sully groaned. "No more shop talk, okay?"

She really didn't have to be coerced, but when he leaned down and delivered a deep, wet kiss, she contritely said, "Okay."

By then they'd nearly reached the bedroom.

She took a final glance over the railing, down at the reception tables and dance floor, then to where the other Steeles were mingling with countless guests. Names of all the people she'd met swirled in Judith's head: there'd been Pansy's sisters, Lily and Vi, as well as their boyfriends, Lou Fairchild and a famous horror novelist who lived on the island.

The ex-mobster, Tommy the Jaw, had magically materialized once there was no longer an all-points bulletin out on him. And Trudy Busey's mother was here, from whom she'd been estranged. Ostensibly, she'd come to cover the wedding for the television station for which she worked, since the story of the Big Apple Bachelors had caught the public imagination. And yet everybody knew she'd really come to be reunited with her daughter.

Judith's eyes settled on Rex and his father. Sully had told her about the rift between the two men, but the events of the past few months had changed things. On this last adventure, Augustus Steele had mellowed, and since he was ready to retire and spend his time fishing, he was glad Rex and Pansy were using their share of the lottery win to refurbish Castle O'Lannaise. Standing near a punch bowl, the two men looked to be demonstrating different techniques for casting fly-fishing rods.

"This place is incredible," Judith said with a sigh as she turned away from the scene. After the *Destiny* exploded, she'd come to Seduction Island on business, and all she'd seen in Castle O'Lannaise was a possible crime scene. Now, with Sully urging her toward their bedroom, she was beginning to see far, far more potential....

"Finally," Sully sighed once they were in the room, and she was trapped beneath him on the round bed. He added, "The dress is beautiful, but..."

"You're going to take it off?" she guessed.

"You're very observant."

"I learned at the police academy."

"You learn a lot in bed, too."

"So do you."

"I try."

He was already dragging the zipper down the curve of her spine and pushing red velvet over her shoulders to reveal a jet-black lace bra and thong set. "But you need not feel alone," he continued huskily, his eyes settling on the scanty scraps of lace, suddenly groaning when nothing more than the heat of his gaze made her nipples pucker.

Her voice caught with excitement. "You were saying I shouldn't worry? That I shouldn't feel alone?"

He shook his head, his amber eyes darkening to a color that reminded her of aged whiskey. "No. I think I might undress, too."

She would have laughed, but desire flooded her as she watched him shrug out of the tux jacket, remove his cummerbund and shirt, exposing the thick, tangled golden hair that covered his chest. "All this," she murmured. "Just to keep me company, so I won't be naked alone. Why, that's so kind of you, Sully Steele."

He was ridding himself of his pants and briefs. "I'm doing this only out of the goodness of my heart," he assured her.

"Me, too." She opened the front clasp of her bra, further excited by the pure male appreciation she saw in his gaze. "You must be a saint."

Naked now, he flashed a grin, and when he spoke, his voice was deeper, ragged with need. "Only when I'm not a sinner." He gave a throaty chuckle as he leaned over the side of the bed and poured two glasses of champagne.

"A toast?" she asked a moment later, surprised when he lifted the bottle instead of the two filled glasses. The flash of his devilish grin should have prepared her, but she gasped as he tilted the bottle twice, liberally splashing the breasts she'd just exposed. Her nipples constricted and she squealed. "What are you doing, Sully?" she demanded breathlessly. "That's cold!"

"Not anymore."

His hot mouth was swiftly on her then, licking all the way down her cleavage. When he glanced up, his smile had turned heartwarming, sly and seductive. "This is payback for this morning."

Bending, he very slowly circled a nipple with his tongue, then moved to the other, creating delicious swirls that made her writhe against him. Biting her lower lip, she held back a moan as long as she could, then released it, and in response, he inhaled sharply. Leaning away a fraction, he scooted downward, this time splashing her belly. Champagne fizzled, bubbling against her bare skin.

Arching, she threaded her hand in his hair as he began lapping from her navel. "Keep it up," she gasped, "and there won't anything left to drink."

"Your belly button doesn't hold that much bubbly," Sully argued.

She merely pulled him upward, toward her, using his silken hair for leverage. When his hips locked with hers, and she could feel him there—hot, hard and throbbing—she whispered, "I want you inside me."

"What the lady wants," he whispered as he slowly entered her, sweeping his lips across hers, "the lady gets."

It was much later when they ran out of champagne. Later still when Sully used her bare back for a desk and they jointly composed a letter about how they'd met and what they'd come to mean to each other. And it was much later still—years, in fact—when that champagne bottle washed up on a faraway shore.

A man was fly-fishing, casting his rod into the breakers, and spying the bottle bobbing in the waves, he lifted it. Sitting in the sand, he uncorked it, pulled out the letter and read the first words:

> Some time ago, my soon-to-be husband wrote a love letter, put it into a bottle and threw it into the Hudson River in New York City.
>
> I found that message and wrote back.
>
> Neither of us really believed we'd ever find true love, but we have, and soon, we plan to exchange our vows on a bridge overlooking Bethesda Fountain in Central Park. And so tonight, after having polished off this bottle of champagne, we decided to write another letter, to say just one thing, in hopes of inspiring lovers everywhere who are still waiting:
>
> Love will find you.

The Masterson brothers—Zane and Grey.
Both gorgeous, both oh-so-sexy.
Identical?

Natural-born lady-killers Zane and Grey Masterson are notorious among the female population of New Orleans for their "love 'em and leave 'em smiling" attitudes. But what happens when they decide to switch places—and each brother finds himself in an intimate struggle with the one woman he can't resist...?

Find out in...

DOUBLE THE PLEASURE by Julie Elizabeth Leto
&
DOUBLE THE THRILL by Susan Kearney

Both books available in August 2002,
wherever Harlequin books are sold.

When these two guys meet their match,
the results are just two sexy!

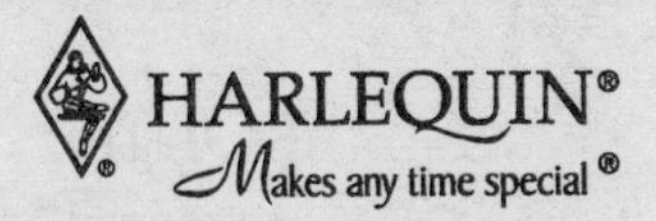

Visit us at www.eHarlequin.com

HBTWINS

Ready to take on the world—and some unsuspecting men—these red-hot royals are looking for love and fun in *all* the right places!

Don't miss four new stories by two of Duets hottest authors!

Once Upon a Tiara

Henry Ever After

by Carrie Alexander
September 2002

A Royal Mess

Her Knight To Remember

by Jill Shalvis
October 2002

Available at your favorite retail outlet.

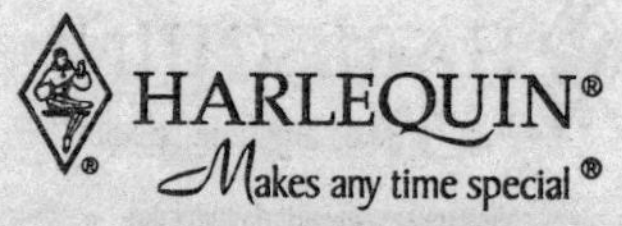

Visit us at www.eHarlequin.com

HDRHR

More fabulous reading from
the Queen of Sizzle!

LORI FOSTER

with

Forever and Always

Back by popular demand are the scintillating stories of Gabe and Jordan Buckhorn. They're gorgeous, sexy and single...at least for now!

Available wherever books are sold—September 2002.

And look for Lori's ***brand-new*** single title,
CASEY in early 2003

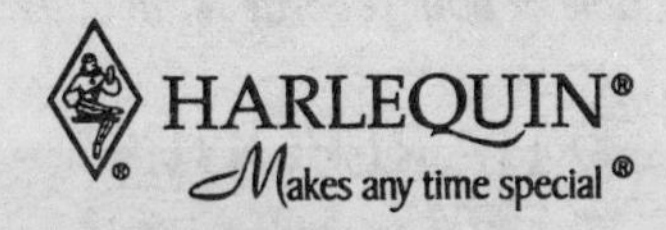

Visit us at www.eHarlequin.com

PHLF-2

buy books

♥ We have your favorite books from Harlequin, Silhouette, MIRA and Steeple Hill, plus bestselling authors in Other Romances. Discover savings, find new releases and fall in love with past classics all over again!

online reads

♥ Read daily and weekly chapters from Internet-exclusive serials, and decide what should happen next in great interactive stories!

magazine

♥ Learn how to spice up your love life, play fun games and quizzes, read about celebrities, travel, beauty and so much more.

authors

♥ Select from over 300 Harlequin author profiles and read interviews with your favorite bestselling authors!

community

♥ Share your passion for love, life and romance novels in our online message boards!

learn to write

♥ All the tips and tools you need to craft the perfect novel, including our special romance novel critique service.

membership

♥ FREE! Be the first to hear about all your favorite themes, authors and series and be part of exciting contests, exclusive promotions, special deals and online events.

Makes any time special®—online...

Visit us at
www.eHarlequin.com

HINT7CH

If you enjoyed what you just read, then we've got an offer you can't resist!

Take 2 bestselling love stories FREE!

Plus get a FREE surprise gift!

Clip this page and mail it to Harlequin Reader Service®

IN U.S.A.	IN CANADA
3010 Walden Ave.	P.O. Box 609
P.O. Box 1867	Fort Erie, Ontario
Buffalo, N.Y. 14240-1867	L2A 5X3

YES! Please send me 2 free Harlequin Temptation® novels and my free surprise gift. After receiving them, if I don't wish to receive anymore, I can return the shipping statement marked cancel. If I don't cancel, I will receive 4 brand-new novels each month, before they're available in stores. In the U.S.A., bill me at the bargain price of $3.57 plus 25¢ shipping and handling per book and applicable sales tax, if any*. In Canada, bill me at the bargain price of $4.24 plus 25¢ shipping and handling per book and applicable taxes**. That's the complete price and a savings of 10% off the cover prices—what a great deal! I understand that accepting the 2 free books and gift places me under no obligation ever to buy any books. I can always return a shipment and cancel at any time. Even if I never buy another book from Harlequin, the 2 free books and gift are mine to keep forever.

142 HDN DNT5
342 HDN DNT6

Name (PLEASE PRINT)

Address Apt.#

City State/Prov. Zip/Postal Code

* Terms and prices subject to change without notice. Sales tax applicable in N.Y.
** Canadian residents will be charged applicable provincial taxes and GST.
All orders subject to approval. Offer limited to one per household and not valid to current Harlequin Temptation® subscribers.
® are registered trademarks of Harlequin Enterprises Limited.

TEMP02 ©1998 Harlequin Enterprises Limited

Attracted to strong, silent cowboys?

Then get ready to meet three of the most irresistibly sexy heroes you've ever met in

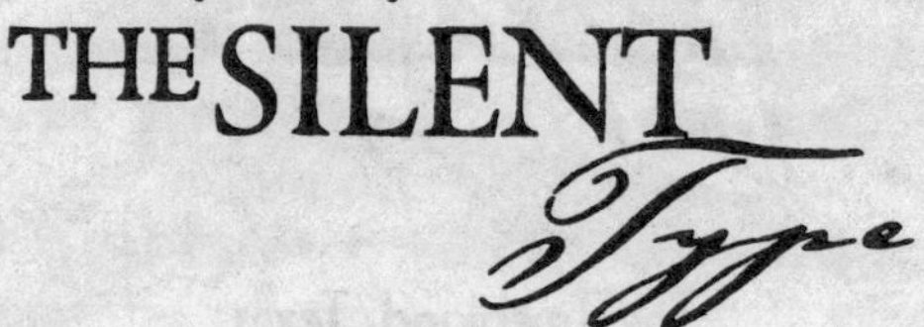

From bestselling Harlequin Temptation® author

VICKI
LEWIS
THOMPSON

These three lonesome cowboys are about to find some *very* interesting company!

Coming to a store near you in August 2002.

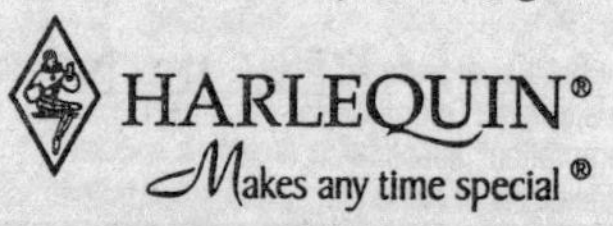

Visit us at www.eHarlequin.com

BR3TST

The Trueblood, Texas
tradition continues in...

HARLEQUIN® Blaze™

TRULY, MADLY, DEEPLY
by Vicki Lewis Thompson
August 2002

Ten years ago, Dustin Ramsey and Erica Mann shared their first sexual experience. It was a disaster. Now Dustin's determined to find—and seduce—Erica again, to prove to her, and himself, that he can do better. Much, *much* better. Only, little does he guess that Erica's got the same agenda....

Don't miss Blaze's next two sizzling Trueblood tales:

EVERY MOVE YOU MAKE by Tori Carrington
September 2002
&
LOVE ON THE ROCKS by Debbi Rawlins
October 2002

Available wherever Harlequin books are sold.

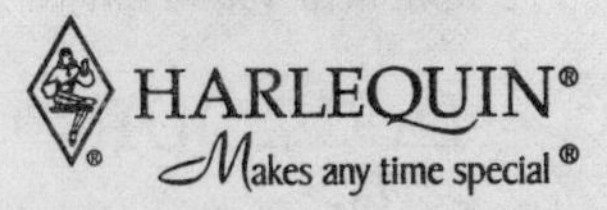

Visit us at www.eHarlequin.com

HBTBT2